C000144322

THE GIRL FROM HOLLYWOOD

Edgar Rice Burroughs

The story alternates between the all-American Pennington family on their remote California ranch and a young girl. She finally confides that she wants to try being an actress before she agrees to settle down on the ranch.

The Pennington's have a beautiful estate, and affectionate relationships with their children, Custer and Eva. Custer has had an "understanding" with neighbour and childhood friend Grace Evans for a long time, but she finally confides that she wants to try being an actress before she agrees to settle down on the ranch. Her brother Guy is an aspiring writer. He has just purchased some bootleg booze, and shares it with Custer, although both Grace and Custer's mother have observed that he has a drinking problem.

Bit-part actress Shannon Burke, known on the screen as Gaza de Lure, remembers her Hollywood history. She had come for fame. She refused to trade sexual favours for work, and found that she could not get better roles. Actor-director Wilson Crumb was the first to behave decently to her, as a gentleman. He got her a contract with his company, and gradually increased his attentions to her.

Finally, he gave her powder, saying it was aspirin, and over several days intentionally got her hooked-on cocaine. To keep her drug supply steady, she angrily agreed to visit him during the day, but refused to live with him, going home each night to her own place. Eventually, she began selling cocaine, morphine and heroin for him.

Custer and Shannon are both arrested. There is a lot of circumstantial evidence against Custer. Shannon's sordid Hollywood past comes out during the trial...

An Evening's "Dramatic Readings"

CHAPTER I

The two horses picked their way carefully downward over the loose shale of the steep hillside. The big bay stallion in the lead sidled mincingly, tossing his head nervously, and flecking the flannel shirt of his rider with foam. Behind the man on the stallion a girl rode a clean-limbed bay of lighter colour, whose method of descent, while less showy, was safer, for he came more slowly, and in the very bad places he braced his four feet forward and slid down, sometimes almost sitting upon the ground.

At the base of the hill there was a narrow level strip; then an eight-foot wash, with steep banks, barred the way to the opposite side of the canyon, which rose gently to the hills beyond. At the foot of the descent the man reined in and waited until the girl was safely down; then he wheeled his mount and trotted toward the wash. Twenty feet from it he gave the animal its head and a word. The horse broke into a gallop, took off at the edge of the wash, and cleared it so effortlessly as almost to give the impression of flying.

Behind the man came the girl, but her horse came at the wash with a rush—not the slow, steady gallop of the stallion—and at the very brink he stopped to gather himself. The dry bank caved beneath his front feet, and into the wash he went, head first.

The man turned and spurred back. The girl looked up from her saddle, making a wry face.

"No damage?" he asked, an expression of concern upon his face.

"No damage," the girl replied. "Senator is clumsy enough at jumping, but no matter what happens he always lights on his feet."

"Ride down a bit," said the man. "There's an easy way out just below."

She moved off in the direction he indicated, her horse picking his way among the loose boulders in the wash bottom.

"Mother says he's part cat," she remarked. "I wish he could jump like the Apache!"

The man stroked the glossy neck of his own mount.

"He never will," he said. "He's afraid. The Apache is absolutely fearless; he'd go anywhere I'd ride him. He's been mired with me twice, but he never refuses a wet spot; and that's a test, I say, of a horse's courage."

They had reached a place where the bank was broken down, and the girl's horse scrambled from the wash.

"Maybe he's like his rider," suggested the girl, looking at the Apache; "brave, but reckless."

"It was worse than reckless," said the man. "It was asinine. I shouldn't have led you over the jump when I know how badly Senator jumps."

"And you wouldn't have, Custer,"—she hesitated— "if—"

"The vultures are back," she said. "I am always glad to see them come again."

"Yes," said the man. "They are bully scavengers, and we don't have to pay 'em wages."

The girl smiled up at him.

"I'm afraid my thoughts were more poetic than practical," she said. "I was only thinking that the sky looked less lonely now that they have come. Why suggest their diet?"

"I know what you mean," he said, "I like them too. Maligned as they are, they are really wonderful birds, and sort of mysterious. Did you ever stop to think that you never see a very young one or a dead one? Where do they die? Where do they grow to maturity? I wonder what they've found up there! Let's ride up. Martin said he saw a new calf up beyond Jackknife Canyon yesterday. That would be just about under where they're circling now."

They guided their horses around a large, flat slab of rock that some camper had contrived into a table beneath the sycamore, and started across the trail toward the opposite side of the canyon.

They were in the middle of the trail when the man drew in and listened.

"Someone is coming," he said, "Let's wait and see who it is. I haven't sent any one back into the hills today."

"I have an idea," remarked the girl, "that there is more going on up there"—she nodded toward the mountains stretching to the south of them—than you know about."

"How is that?" he asked.

"So often recently we have heard horsemen passing the ranch late at night. If they weren't going to stop at your place, those who rode up the trail must have been headed into the high hills; but I'm sure that those whom we heard coming down weren't coming from the Rancho del Ganado."

"No," he said, "not late at night—or not often, at any rate."

The footsteps of a cantering horse drew rapidly closer, and presently the animal and its rider came into view around a turn in the trail.

"It's only Allen," said the girl.

The newcomer reined in at sight of the man and the girl. He was evidently surprised, and the girl thought that he seemed ill at ease.

"Just givin' Baldy a work-out," he explained. "He ain't been out for three or four days, an' you told me to work 'em out if I had time."

Custer Pennington nodded.

"See any stock back there?"

"No. How's the Apache today—forgin' as bad as usual?"

Pennington shook his head negatively.

"That fellow shod him yesterday just the way I want him shod. I wish you'd take a good look at his shoes, Slick, so you can see that he's always shod this same way." His eyes had been traveling over Slick's mount, whose heaving sides were covered with lather. "Baldy's pretty soft, Slick; I wouldn't work him too hard all at once. Get him up to it gradually."

He turned and rode off with the girl at his side. Slick Allen looked after them for a moment and then moved his horse off at a slow walk toward the ranch. He was a lean, sinewy man, of medium height. He might have been a cavalryman once. He sat his horse, even at a walk, like one who has sweated and bled under a drill sergeant in the days of his youth.

"How do you like him?" the girl asked of Pennington.

"He's a good horseman, and good horsemen are getting rare these days," replied Pennington; "but I don't know that I'd choose him for a playmate. Don't you like him?"

"I'm afraid I don't. His eyes give me the creeps—they're like a fish's."

"To tell the truth, Grace I don't like him," said Custer. "He's one of those rare birds—a good horseman who doesn't love horses. I imagine he won't last long on the Rancho del Ganado; but we've got to give him a fair shake—he's only been with us a few weeks."

They were picking their way toward the summit of a steep hogback. The man, who led, was seeking carefully for the safest footing, shamed out of his recent recklessness by the thought of how close the girl had come to a serious accident through his thoughtlessness. They rode along the hogback until they could look down into a tiny basin where a small bunch of cattle was grazing, and then, turning and dipping over the edge, they dropped slowly toward the animals.

Near the bottom of the slope they came upon a white-faced bull standing beneath the spreading shade of alive oak. He turned his woolly face toward them, his red-rimmed eyes observing them dispassionately for a moment. Then he turned away again and resumed his cud, disdaining further notice of them.

"That's the King of Ganado, isn't it?" asked the girl.

"Looks like him, doesn't he? But he isn't. He's the King's likeliest son, and unless I'm mistaken he's going to give the old fellow a mighty tough time of it this fall, if the old boy wants to hang on to the grand championship. We've never shown him yet. It's an idea of father's. He's always wanted to spring a new champion at a great show and surprise the world. He's kept this fellow hidden away ever since he gave the first indication that he was going to be a fine bull. At least a hundred breeders have visited the herd in the past year, and not one of them has seen him. Father says he's the greatest bull that ever lived, and that his first show is going to be the International."

"I just know he'll win," exclaimed the girl. "Why look at him! Isn't he a beauty?"

"Got a back like a billiard table," commented Custer proudly.

They rode down among the heifers. There were a dozen beauties—three-year-olds. Hidden to one side, behind a small bush, the man's quick eyes discerned a little bundle of red and white.

"There it is, Grace," he called, and the two rode toward it.

One of the heifers looked fearfully toward them, then at the bush, and finally walked toward it, lowing plaintively.

"We're not going to hurt it, little girl," the man assured her.

As they came closer, there arose a thing of long, wobbly legs, big joints, and great, dark eyes, its spotless coat of red and white shining with health and life.

"The cunning thing!" cried the girl. "How I'd like to squeeze it! I just love 'em, Custer!"

She had slipped from her saddle, and, dropping her reins on the ground, was approaching the calf.

"Look out for the cow!" cried the man, as he dismounted and moved forward to the girl's side, with his arm through the Apache's reins. "She hasn't been up much, and she may be a little wild."

The calf stood its ground for a moment, and then, with tail erect, cavorted madly for its mother, behind whom it took refuge.

"I just love 'em! I just love 'em! repeated the girl.

"You say the same thing about the colts and the little pigs," the man reminded her.

"I love 'em all!" she cried, shaking her head, her eyes twinkling.

"You love them because they're little and helpless, just like babies," he said. "Oh, Grace, how you'd love a baby!"

The girl flushed prettily. Quite suddenly he seized her in his arms and crushed her to him, smothering her with a long kiss. Breathless, she wriggled partially away, but he still held her in his arms.

"Why won't you, Grace?" he begged. "There'll never be anybody else for me or for you. Father and mother and Eva love you almost as much as I do, and on your side your mother and Guy have always seemed to take it as a matter of course that we'd marry. It isn't the drinking, is it, dear?"

"No, it's not that, Custer. Of course I'll marry you—someday; but not yet. Why, I haven't lived, yet, Custer! I want to live. I want to do something outside of the humdrum life that I have always led and the humdrum life that I shall live as a wife and mother. I want to live a little, Custer, and then I'll be ready to settle down. You all tell me that I am beautiful, and down, away in the depth of my soul, I feel that I have talent. If I have, I ought to use the gifts God has given me."

She was speaking very seriously, and the man listened patiently and with respect, for he realized that she was revealing for the first time a secret yearning that she must have long held locked in her bosom.

"Just what do you want to do, dear?" he asked gently.

"I—oh, it seems silly when I try to put it in words, but in dreams it is very beautiful and very real."

"The stage?" he asked.

"It is just like you to understand!" Her smile rewarded him. "Will you help me? I know mother will object."

"You want me to help you take all the happiness out of my life?" he asked.

"It would only be for a little while just a few years, and then I would come back to you—after I had made good."

CHAPTER II

The man bent his lips to hers again, and her arms stole about his neck. The calf, in the meantime, perhaps disgusted by such absurdities, had scampered off to try his brand-new legs again, with the result that he ran into a low bush, turned a somersault, and landed on his back. The mother, still doubtful of the intentions of the newcomers, to whose malevolent presence she may have attributed the accident, voiced a perturbed low; whereupon there broke from the vicinity of the live oak a deep note, not unlike the rumbling of distant thunder.

The man looked up.

"I think we'll be going," he said. "The Emperor has issued an ultimatum."

"Or a bull, perhaps," Grace suggested, as they walked quickly toward her horse.

"Awful!" he commented, as he assisted her into the saddle.

Then he swung to his own.

The Emperor moved majestically toward them, his nose close to the ground. Occasionally he stopped, pawing the earth and throwing dust upon his broad back.

"Doesn't he look wicked?" cried the girl. "Just look at those eyes!"

"He's just an old bluffer," replied the man. "However, I'd rather have you in the saddle, for you can't always be sure just what they'll do. We must call his bluff, though; it would never do to run from him—might give him bad habits."

He rode toward the advancing animal, breaking into a canter as he drew near the bull, and striking his booted leg with a quirt.

"Hi, there, you old reprobate! Beat it!" he cried.

The bull stood his ground with lowered head and rumbled threats until the horseman was almost upon him; then he turned quickly aside as the rider went past.

"That's better," remarked Custer, as the girl joined him.

"You're not a bit afraid of him, are you, Custer? You're not afraid of anything."

"Oh, I wouldn't say that," he demurred. "I learned a long time ago that most encounters consist principally of bluff. Maybe I've just grown to be a good bluffer. Anyhow, I'm a better bluffer than the Emperor. If the rascal had only known it, he could have run me ragged."

As they rode up the side of the basin, the man's eyes moved constantly from point to point, now noting the condition of the pasture grasses, or again searching the more distant hills. Presently they alighted upon a thin, wavering line of brown, which zigzagged down the opposite side of the basin from a clump of heavy brush that partially hid a small ravine, and crossed the meadow ahead of them.

"There's a new trail, Grace, and it don't belong there. Let's go and take a look at it."

They rode ahead until they reached the trail, at a point where it crossed the bottom of the basin and started up the side they had been ascending. The man leaned above his horse's shoulder and examined the trampled turf.

"Horses," he said. "I thought so, and it's been used a lot this winter. You can see even now where the animals slipped and floundered after the heavy rains."

"But you don't run horses in this pasture, do you?" asked the girl.

"No; and we haven't run anything in it since last summer. This is the only bunch in it, and they were just turned in about a week ago. Anyway the horses that made this trail were mostly shod. Now what in the world is anybody going up there for?" His eyes wandered to the heavy brush into which the trail disappeared upon the opposite rim of the basin. "I'll have to follow that up to-morrow—it's too late to do it to-day."

"We can follow it the other way, toward the ranch," she suggested.

They found the trail wound up the hillside and crossed the hogback in heavy brush, which, in many places, had been cut away to allow the easier passage of a horseman.

"Do you see," asked Custer, as they drew rein at the summit of the ridge, "that although the trail crosses here in plain sight of the ranch house, the brush would absolutely conceal a horseman from the view of any one at the house? It must run right down into Jackknife Canyon. Funny none of us have noticed it, for there's scarcely a week that that trail isn't ridden by some of us!"

As they descended into the canyon, they discovered why that end of the new trail had not been noticed. It ran deep and well marked through the heavy brush of a gully to a place where the brush commenced to thin, and there it branched into a dozen dim trails that joined and blended with the old, well worn cattle paths of the hillside.

"Somebody's might foxy," observed the man; "but I don't see what it's all about. The days of cattle runners and bandits are over."

"Just imagine!" exclaimed the girl. "A real mystery in our lazy, old hills!"

The man rode in silence and in thought. A herd of pure-bred Herefords, whose value would have ransomed half the crowned heads remaining in Europe, grazed in the several pastures that ran far back into those hills; and back there somewhere that trail led, but for what purpose? No good purpose, he was sure, or it had not been so cleverly hidden.

As they came to the trail which they called the Camino Corto, where it commenced at the gate leading from the old goat corral, the man jerked his thumb toward the west along it

"They must come and go this way," he said.

"Perhaps they're the ones mother and I have heard passing at night," suggested the girl. "If they are, they come right through your property, below the house— not this way."

He opened the gate from the saddle, and they passed through, crossing the barranco, and stopping for a moment to look at the pigs and talk with the herdsman. Then they rode on toward the ranch house, a half mile farther down the widening canyon. It stood upon the summit of a low hill, the declining sun transforming its plastered walls, its cupolas, the sturdy arches of its arcades, into the semblance of a Moorish castle.

At the foot of the hill they dismounted at the saddle horse stable, tied their horses, and ascended the long flight of rough concrete steps toward the house. As they rounded the wild sumac bush at the summit, they were espied by those sitting in the patio, around three sides of which the house was built.

"Oh, here they are now!" exclaimed Mrs. Pennington. "We were so afraid that Grace would ride right on home, Custer. We had just persuaded Mrs. Evans to stay for dinner. Guy is coming, too."

"Mother, you here, too?" cried the girl. "How nice and cool it is in here. It would save a lot of trouble if we brought our things, mother."

"We are hoping that at least one of you will, very soon," said Colonel Pennington, who had risen, and now put an arm affectionately about the girl's shoulders.

"That's what I've been telling her again this afternoon," said Custer; "but instead she wants to—"

The girl turned toward him with a little frown and shake of her head.

"You'd better run down and tell Allen that we won't use the horses until after dinner," she said.

He grimaced good-naturedly and turned away.

"I'll have him take Senator home," he said. "I can drive you and your mother down in the car, when you leave."

As he descended the steps that wound among the umbrella trees, taking on their new foliage, he saw Allen examining the Apache's shoes. As he neared them, the horse pulled away from the man, his suddenly lowered hoof striking Allen's instep. With an oath the fellow stepped back and swung a vicious kick to the animal's belly. Almost simultaneously a hand fell heavily upon his shoulder. He was jerked roughly back, whirled about, and sent spinning a dozen feet away, where he stumbled and fell. As he scrambled to his feet, white with rage, he saw the younger Pennington before him.

"Go to the office and get your time," ordered Pennington.

"I'll get you first, you son of a—"

A hard fist connecting suddenly with his chin put a painful period to his sentence before it was completed, and stopped his mad rush.

"I'd be more careful of my conversation, Allen, if I were you," said Pennington quietly. "Just because you've been drinking is no excuse for that. Now go on up to the office as I told you to."

He had caught the odor of whiskey as he jerked the man past him.

"You goin' to can me for drinkin'—you?" demanded Allen.

"You know what I'm canning you for. You know that's the one thing that don't go on Ganado. You ought to get what you gave the Apache, and you'd better beat it before I lose my temper and give it to you!"

The man rose slowly to his feet. In his mind he was revolving his chances of successfully renewing his attack; but presently his judgment got the better of his desire and his rage. He moved off slowly up the hill toward the house. A few yards, and he turned.

"I ain't a goin' to ferget this, you—you—"

"Be careful!" Pennington admonished.

"Nor you ain't goin' to ferget it, neither, you foxtrottin' dude!"

Allen turned again to the ascent of the steps. Pennington walked to the Apache and stroked his muzzle.

"Old boy," he crooned, "there don't anybody kick you and get away with it, does there?"

Halfway up, Allen stopped and turned again.

"You think you're the whole cheese, you Penningtons, don't you?" he called back. "With all your money an' your fine friends! Fine friends, yah! I can put one of 'em where he belongs any time I want—the darn bootlegger! That's what he is. You wait— you'll see!"

"A-ah beat it!" sighed Pennington wearily.

Mounting the Apache, he led Grace's horse along the foot of the hill toward the smaller ranch house of their neighbor, some half mile away. Humming a little tune, he unsaddled Senator, turned him into his corral, saw that there was water in his trough, and emptied a measure of oats into his manger, for the horse had cooled off since the afternoon ride. As neither of the Evans ranch hands appeared, he found a piece of rag and wiped off the Senator's bit, turned the saddle blankets wet side up to dry, and then, leaving the stable, crossed the yard to mount the Apache.

A young man in riding clothes appeared simultaneously from the interior of the bungalow, which stood a hundred feet away. Crossing the wide porch, he called to Pennington.

"Hello there, Penn! What are you doing?" he demanded.

"Just brought Senator in— Grace is up at the house. You're coming up there, too, Guy."

"Sure, but come in here a second. I've got something to show you."

Pennington crossed the yard and entered the house behind Grace's brother, who conducted him to his bedroom. Here young Evans unlocked a closet, and, after rummaging behind some clothing, emerged with a bottle, the shape and dimensions of which were once as familiar in the land of the free as the benign countenance of Lydia E. Pinkham.

"It's the genuine stuff, Penn, too!" he declared.

Pennington smiled.

"Thanks, old fellow, but I've quit," he said.

"Quit!" exclaimed Evans.

"Yep."

"But think of it, man—aged eight years in the wood, and bottled in bond before July 1, 1919. The real thing, and as cheap as moonshine— only six beans a quart. Can you believe it?"

"I cannot," admitted Pennington. "Your conversation listens phoney."

"But it's truth. You may have quit, but one little snifter of this won't hurt you. Here's this bottle already open just try it"; and he proffered the bottle and a glass to the other.

"Well, it's pretty hard to resist anything that sounds as good as this does," remarked Pennington. "I guess one won't hurt me any." He poured himself a drink and took it. "Wonderful!" he ejaculated.

"Here," said Evans, diving into the closet once more. "I got you a bottle, too, and we can get more."

Pennington took the bottle and examined it, almost caressingly.

"Eight years in the wood!" he murmured. "I've got to take it, Guy. Must have something to hand down to posterity." He drew a bill fold from his pocket and counted out six dollars.

"Thanks," said Guy. "You'll never regret it."

CHAPTER III

As the two young men climbed the hill to the big house, a few minutes later, they found the elder Pennington standing at the edge of the driveway that circled the hill top, looking out toward the wide canyon and the distant mountains. In the nearer foreground lay the stable and corrals of the saddle horses, the hen house with its two long alfalfa runways, and the small dairy barn accommodating the little herd of Guernseys that supplied milk, cream, and butter for the ranch. A quarter of a mile beyond, among the trees, was the red-roofed "cabin" where the unmarried ranch hands ate and slept, near the main corrals with their barns, outhouses, and sheds.

The two young men joined the older, and Custer put an arm affectionately about his father's shoulders.

"You never tire of it," said the young man.

"I have been looking at it for twenty-two years, my son," replied the elder Pennington, "and each year it has become more wonderful to me. It never changes, and yet it is never twice alike. See the purple sage away off there, and the lighter spaces of wild buckwheat, and here and there among the scrub oak the beautiful pale green of the manzanita—scintillant jewels in the diadem of the hills! And the faint haze of the mountains that seem to throw them just a little out of focus, to make them a perfect background for the beautiful hills which the Supreme Artist is placing on his canvas today. An hour from now He will paint another masterpiece, and to-night another, and forever others, with never two alike, nor ever one that mortal man can duplicate; and all for us, boy, all for us, if we have the hearts and the souls to see!"

"How you love it!" said the boy.

"Yes, and your mother loves it; and it is our great happiness that you and Eva love it, too."

The boy made no reply. He did love it; but his was the heart of youth, and it yearned for change and for adventure and for what lay beyond the circling hills and the broad, untroubled valley that spread its level fields below "the castle on the hill."

"The girls are dressing for a swim," said the older man, after a moment of silence. "Aren't you boys going in?"

"The girls" included his wife and Mrs. Evans, as well as Grace, for the colonel insisted that youth was purely a physical and mental attribute, independent of time. If one could feel and act in accord with the spirit of youth, one could not be old.

"Are you going in?" asked his son.

"Yes. I was waiting for you two."

"I think I'll be excused, sir," said Guy. "The water is too cold yet. I tried it yesterday, and nearly froze to death. I'll come and watch."

The two Penningtons moved off toward the house, to get into swimming things, while young Evans wandered down into the water gardens. As he stood there, idly content in the quiet beauty of the spot, Allen came down the steps, his check in his hand. At sight of the boy he halted behind him, an unpleasant expression upon his face.

Evans, suddenly aware that he was not alone, turned and recognized the man.

"Oh, hello, Allen!" he said.

"Young Pennington just canned me," said Allen, with no other return of Evan's greeting.

"I'm sorry," said Evans.

"You may be sorrier!" growled Allen, continuing on his way toward the cabin to get his blankets and clothes.

For a moment Guy stared after the man, a puzzled expression knitting his brows. Then he slowly flushed, glancing quickly about to see if any one had overheard the brief conversation between Slick Allen and himself.

A few minutes later he entered the enclosure west of the house, where the swimming pool lay. Mrs. Pennington and her guests were already in the pool, swimming vigorously to keep warm, and a moment later the colonel and Custer ran from the house and dived in simultaneously. Though there was twenty-six years' difference in their ages, it was not evidenced by any lesser vitality or agility on the part of the older man.

Colonel Custer Pennington had been born in Virginia fifty years before. Graduated from the Virginia Military Institute and West Point, he had taken a commission in the cavalry branch of the service. Campaigning in Cuba, he had been shot through one lung, and shortly after the close of the war he was retired for disability, with rank of lieutenant-colonel. In 1900 he had come to California, on the advice of his physician in the forlorn hope that he might prolong his sufferings a few years more.

And so Pennington had come West with Mrs. Pennington and little Custer, Jr., and had found the Rancho del Ganado run down, untenanted and for sale.

He judged from the soil and the water that Ganado was not well suited to raise the type of horse that he knew best, and that he and his father and his grandfathers before them had bred in Virginia; but he saw other possibilities. Moreover, he loved the hills and the canyons from the first; and so he had purchased the ranch, more to have something that would temporarily occupy his mind until his period of exile was ended by a return to his native State, or by death, than with any idea that it would prove a permanent home.

CHAPTER IV

Work and play were inextricably entangled upon Ganado, the play being of a nature that fitted them better for their work, while the work, always in the open and usually from the saddle, they enjoyed fully as much as the play. While the tired business man of the city was expending a day's vitality and nervous energy in an effort to escape from the turmoil of the mad rush-hour and find a strap from which to dangle homeward amid the toxic effluvia of the melting pot, Colonel Pennington plunged and swam in the cold, invigorating waters of his pool, after a day of labor fully as constructive and profitable as theirs.

"One more dive!" he called, balancing upon the end of the springboard, "and then I'm going out. Eva ought to be here by the time we're dressed, hadn't she? I'm about famished."

"I haven't heard the train whistle yet, though it must be due," replied Mrs. Pennington. "You and Boy make so much noise swimming that we'll miss Gabriel's trumpet if we happen to be in the pool at the time!"

They were still bantering as they entered the house and sought their several rooms to dress.

Guy Evans strolled from the walled garden of the swimming pool to the open arch that broke the long pergola beneath which the driveway ran along the north side of the house. Here he had an unobstructed view of the broad valley stretching away to the mountains in the distance. Down the center of the valley a toy train moved noiselessly. As he watched it, he saw a puff of white rise from the tiny engine. It rose and melted in the evening air before the thin, clear sound of the whistle reached his ears. The train crawled behind the green of trees and disappeared.

He knew that it had stopped at the station, and that a slender, girlish figure was alighting, with a smile for the porter and a gay word for the conductor who had carried her back and forth for years upon her occasional visits to the city a hundred miles away. Now the chauffeur was taking her bag and carrying it to the roadster that she would drive home along the wide, straight boulevard that crossed the valley—utterly ruining a number of perfectly good speed laws.

The headlights of a motor car turned in at the driveway. Guy went to the east porch and looked in at the living room door, where some of the family had already collected. "Eva's coming!" he announced.

With a rush the car topped the hill, swung up the driveway, and stopped at the corner of the house. A door flew open, and the girl leaped from the driver's seat. "Hello, everybody!" she cried.

Snatching a kiss from her brother as she passed him, she fairly leaped upon her mother hugging, kissing, laughing, dancing, and talking all at once. Espying her father, she relinquished a disheveled and laughing mother and dived for him.

"Most adorable pops!" she cried, as he caught her in his arms. "Are you glad to have your little nuisance back? I'll bet you're not. Do you love me? You won't when you know how much I've spent, but oh, popsy, I had such a good time! That's all there was to it, and oh, momsie, who, who, who do you suppose I met? Oh, you'd never guess—never, never!"

"Whom did you meet?" asked her mother.

"Yes, little one, whom did you meet?" inquired her brother.

"And he's perfectly gorgeous, " continued the girl, as if there had been no interruption; "and I danced with him—oh, such divine dancing! Oh, Guy Evans! Why how do you do? I never saw you."

The young man nodded glumly.

"How are you, Eva?" he said.

"Mrs. Evans is here, too, dear," her mother reminded her.

The girl curtsied before her mother's guest, and then threw her arm about the older woman's neck.

"Oh, Aunt Mae!" she cried. "I'm so excited; but you should have seen him, and, momsie, I got the cutest riding hat!" They were moving toward the living room door, which Guy was holding open. "Guy, I got you the splendiferousest Christmas present!"

"Help!" cried her brother, collapsing into a porch chair. "Don't you know that I have a weak heart? Do your Christmas shopping early—do it in April! Oh, Lord, can you beat it?" he demanded of the others. "Can you beat it?"

The colonel was glancing over the headlines of an afternoon paper that Eva had brought from the city.

"What's new?" asked Custer.

"Same old rot," replied his father. "Murders, divorces, kidnappers, bootleggers, and they haven't even the originality to make them interesting by evolving new methods. Oh, hold on—this isn't so bad! 'Two hundred thousand dollars' worth of stolen whiskey landed on coast," he read. 'Prohibition enforcement agents, together with special agents from the Treasury Department, are working on a unique theory that may reveal the whereabouts of the fortune in bonded whiskey stolen from a government warehouse in New York a year ago. All that was known until recently was that the whiskey was removed from the warehouse in trucks in broad daylight, compassing one of the boldest robberies ever committed in New York. Now, from a source which they refuse to divulge, the government sleuths have received information which leads them to believe that the liquid loot was loaded aboard a sailing vessel, and after a long trip around the Horn, is lying somewhere off the coast of southern California. That it is being lightered ashore in launches and transported to some hiding place in the mountains is one theory upon which the government is working. The whiskey is eleven years old, was bottled in bond three years ago, just before the Eighteenth Amendment became a harrowing reality. It will go hard with the traffickers in this particular parcel of wet goods if they are apprehended, since the theft was directly from a government bonded warehouse, and all government officials concerned in the search are anxious to make an example of the guilty parties.'

"Eleven years old!" sighed the colonel. "It makes my mouth water! I've been subsisting on home-made grape wine for over a year. Think of it— a Pennington! Why my ancestors must be writhing in their Virginia graves!"

"On the contrary, they're probably laughing in their sleeves. They died before July 1, 1919," interposed Custer." "Eleven years old-eight years in the wood," he mused aloud, shooting a quick glance in the direction of Guy Evans, who suddenly became deeply interested in a novel lying on a table beside his chair, notwithstanding the fact that he had read it six months before and hadn't liked it. "And it will go hard with the traffickers, too," continued young Pennington. "Well, I should hope it would. They'll probably hang 'em, the vile miscreants!"

Guy had risen and walked to the doorway opening upon the patio.

"I wonder what is keeping Eva," he remarked.

"Getting hungry?" asked Mrs. Pennington. "Well, I guess we all are. Suppose we don't wait any longer? Eva won't mind."

They had finished their soup before Eva joined them, and after the men were reseated they took up the conversation where it had been interrupted.

During a brief moment when she was not engaged in conversation, Guy seized the opportunity to whisper to Eva, who sat next to him.

"Who was that bird you met in L. A.?" he asked.

"Which one?"

"Which one! How many did you meet?"

"Oodles of them."

"I mean the one you were ranting about."

"Which one was I ranting about? I don't remember."

"You're enough to drive anybody to drink, Eva Pennington!" cried the young man disgustedly.

"Radiant man!" she cooed. "What's the dapper little idea in that talented brain jealous?"

"I want to know who he is," demanded Guy.

"Who who is?"

"You know perfectly well who I mean—the poor fish you were raving about before dinner. You said you danced with him. Who is he? That's what I want to know."

"I don't like the way you talk to me; but if you must know, he was the most dazzling thing you ever saw. He—"

"I never saw him, I don't want to, and I don't care how dazzling he is. I only want to know his name."

"Well, why didn't you say so in the first place? His name's Wilson Crumb." Her tone was as of one who says: "Behold Alexander the Great!"

"Wilson Crumb! Who's he?"

"Do you mean to sit there and tell me that you don't know who Wilson Crumb is, Guy Evans?" she demanded.

"Never heard of him," he insisted.

"Never heard of Wilson Crumb, the famous actor-director? Such ignorance!"

"Did you ever hear of him before this trip to L.A?" inquired her brother from across the table. "I never heard you mention him before."

"Well, maybe I didn't," admitted the girl; "but he's the most dazzling dancer you ever saw—and such eyes! And maybe he'll come out to the ranch and bring his company. He said they were often looking for such locations."

"And I suppose you invited him?" demanded Custer accusingly.

"And why not? I had to be polite, didn't I?"

"You know perfectly well that father has never permitted such a thing," insisted her brother, looking toward the colonel for support.

"He didn't ask father—he asked me," returned the girl.

"You see," said the colonel, "how simply Eva solves every little problem."

"But you know, popsy, how perfectly superb it would be to have them take some pictures right here on our very own ranch, where we could watch them all day long."

"Yes," growled Custer; "watch them wreck the furniture and demolish the lawns! Why, one bird of a director ran a troop of cavalry over one of the finest lawns in Hollywood. Then they'll go up in the hills and chase the cattle over the top into the ocean. I've heard all about them. I'd never allow one of 'em on the place."

"Maybe they're not all inconsiderate and careless," suggested Mrs. Pennington.

"You remember there was a company took a few scenes at my place a year or so ago," interjected Mrs. Evans. "They were very nice indeed."

"They were just wonderful," said Grace Evans. "I hope the colonel lets them come. It would be piles of fun!"

"You can't tell anything about them," volunteered Guy. "I understand they pick up all sorts of riffraff for extra people—I.W.'s and all sorts of people like that. I'd be afraid."

He shook his head dubiously.

"The trouble with you two is," asserted Eva, "that you're afraid to let us girls see any nice-looking actors from the city. That's what's the matter with you!"

"Yes, they're jealous," agreed Mrs. Pennington, laughing.

"Well," said Custer, "if there are leading men there are leading ladies, and from what I've seen of them the leading ladies are better-looking than the leading men. By all means, now that I consider the matter, let them come. Invite them at once, for a month—wire them!"

"Silly!" cried his sister. "He may not come here at all. He just mentioned it casually."

"And all this tempest in a teapot for nothing," said the colonel.

Wilson Crumb was forthwith dropped from the conversation and forgotten by all, even by impressionable little Eva.

As the young people gathered around Mrs. Pennington at the piano in the living room, Mrs. Evans and Colonel Pennington sat apart, carrying on a desultory conversation while they listened to the singing.

"We have a new neighbor," remarked Mrs. Evans, "on the ten-acre orchard adjoining us on the west."

"Yes—Mrs. Burke. She has moved in, has she?" inquired the colonel.

"Yesterday. She is a widow from the East—has a daughter in Los Angeles, I believe."

"She came to see me about a month ago," said the colonel, "to ask my advice about the purchase of the property. She seemed rather a refined, quiet little body, I must tell Julia— she will want to call on her."

"I insisted on her taking dinner with us last night," said Mrs. Evans. "She seems very frail, and was all worn out. Unpacking and settling is trying enough for a robust person, and she seems so delicate that I really don't see how she stood it all."

CHAPTER V

The bungalow at 1421 Vista del Paso was of the new school of Hollywood architecture, which appears to be an hysterical effort to combine Queen Anne, Italian, Swiss chalet, Moorish, Mission, and Martian. You are ushered directly into a living room, whereupon you forget all about architects and art, for the room is really beautiful, even though a trifle heavy in an Oriental way, with its Chinese rugs, dark hangings, and ponderous, overstuffed furniture. Across from you, on a divan, a woman is lying, her face buried among pillows. When you cough, she raises her face toward you, and you see that it is very beautiful, even though the eyes are a bit wide and staring and the expression somewhat haggard. You see a mass of black hair surrounding a face of perfect contour. Even the plucked and pencilled brows, the rouged cheeks, and carmined lips cannot hide a certain dignity and sweetness.

"The same as usual?" she asks in a weary voice.

Your throat is very dry. You swallow before you assure her eagerly, almost feverishly, that her surmise is correct. She leaves the room. Probably you have not noticed that she is wild-eyed and haggard or that her fingers are stained and trembling, for you, too, are wild-eyed and haggard, and you are trembling worse than she.

Presently she returns. In her left hand is a small glass phial, containing many little tablets. As she crosses to you, she extends her right hand with the palm up. It is a slender, delicate hand, yet there is a look of strength to it, for all its whiteness. You lay a bill in it, and she hands you the phial. That is all. You leave, and she closes the Oregon pine door quietly behind you.

As she turns about toward the divan again, she hesitates. Her eyes wander to a closed door at one side of the room. She takes a half step toward it, and then draws back, her shoulders against the door. Her fingers are clenched tightly, the nails sinking into the soft flesh of her palms; but still her eyes are upon the closed door. They are staring and wild, like those of a beast at bay. She is trembling from head to foot.

For a minute she stands there, fighting her grim battle, alone and without help. Then, as with a last mighty efforts, she drags her eyes from the closed door and glances toward the divan. With unsteady step she returns to it and throws herself down among the pillows.

Suddenly she leaps to her feet and rushes toward the mantel.

"Damn you!" she screams, and, seizing the clock, dashes it to pieces upon the tiled hearth.

Then her eyes leap to the closed door; and now, without any hesitation, almost defiantly, she crosses the room, opens the door, and disappears within the bathroom beyond.

Five minutes later the door opens again, and the woman comes back into the living room. She is humming a gay little tune. Stopping at a table, she takes a cigarette from a carved wooden box and lights it. Then she crosses to the baby grand piano in one corner and commences to play. Her voice, rich and melodious, rises in a sweet old song of love and youth and happiness.

Something has mended her shattered nerves. Upon the hearth lies the shattered clock. It can never be mended.

Her name—her professional name—is Gaza de Lure. You may have seen her in small parts on the screen, and may have wondered why some one did not star her. Two years ago she came to Hollywood from a little town in the Middle West—that is, two years before you looked in upon her at the bungalow on the Vista del Paso. She was fired by high purpose then. Her child's heart, burning with lofty ambition, had set its desire upon a noble goal. The broken bodies of a thousand other children dotted the road to the same goal, but she did not see them, or seeing, did not understand.

Stronger, perhaps, than her desire for fame was an unselfish ambition that centered about the mother whom she had left behind. To that mother the girl's success would mean greater comfort and happiness than she had known since a worthless husband had deserted her shortly after the baby came— the baby who was now known as Gaza de Lure.

There had been the usual rounds of the studios, the usual disappointments, followed by more or less regular work as an extra girl. During this period she had learned many things—of some of which she had never thought as having any possible bearing upon her chances for success.

For example, a director had asked her to go with him to Vernon one evening, for dinner and dancing, and she had refused, for several reasons—one being her certainty that her mother would disapprove, and another the fact that the director was a married man. The following day the girl who had accompanied him was cast for a part which had been promised to Gaza, and for which Gaza was peculiarly suited.

In the months that followed she had had many similar experiences, until she had become hardened enough to feel the sense of shame and insult less strongly than at first. She could talk back to them now, and tell them what she thought of them; but she found that she got fewer and fewer engagements. There was always enough to feed and clothe her, and to pay for the little room she rented; but there seemed to be no future, and that had been all that she cared about.

And then she had met Wilson Crumb. She had had a small part in a picture in which he played lead, and which he also directed. He had been very kind to her, very courteous. She had thought him handsome, notwithstanding a certain weakness in his face; but what had attracted her most was the uniform courtesy of his attitude toward all the women of the company. Here at last she thought, she had found a real gentleman whom she could trust implicitly; and once again her ambition lifted its drooping head.

The first picture finished, Crumb had cast her for a more important part in another, and she had made good in both. Before the second picture was completed, the company that employed Crumb offered her a five-year contract. It was only for fifty dollars a week; but it included a clause which automatically increased the salary to one hundred a week, two hundred and fifty, and then five hundred dollars in the event that they starred her. She knew that it was to Crumb that she owed the contract—Crumb had seen to that.

Very gradually, then—so gradually and insidiously that the girl could never recall just when it had started—Crumb commenced to make love to her. At first it took only the form of minor attentions— little courtesies and thoughtful acts; but after a while he spoke of love —very gently and very tenderly, as any man might have done.

She had never thought of loving him or any other man; so she was puzzled at first, but she was not offended. He had given her no cause for offense. When he had first broached the subject, she had asked him not to speak of it, as she did not think that she loved him, and he had said he would wait; but the seed was planted in her mind, and it came to occupy much of her thoughts.

She realized that she owed to him what little success she had achieved. She had an assured income that was sufficient for her simple wants, while permitting her to send something home to her mother every week, and it was all due to the kindness of Wilson Crumb. He was a successful director, he was more than a fair actor, he was good-looking, he was kind, he was a gentleman, and he loved her. What more could any girl ask?

She thought the matter out very carefully, finally deciding that though she did not exactly love Wilson Crumb she probably would learn to love him, and that if he loved her it was in a way her duty to make him happy, when he had done so much for her happiness. She made up her mind, therefore, to marry him whenever he asked her, but Crumb did not ask her to marry him. He continued to make love to her; but the matter of marriage never seemed to enter the conversation.

Once, when they were out on location, and had had a hard day, ending by getting thoroughly soaked in a sudden rain, he had followed her to her room in the little mountain inn where they were stopping.

"You're cold and wet and tired," he said. "I want to give you something that will brace you up."

He entered the room and closed the door behind him. Then he took from his pocket a small piece of paper folded into a package about an inch and three-quarters long by half an inch wide, with one end tucked ingeniously inside the fold to form a fastening. Opening it, he revealed a white powder, the minute crystals of which glistened beneath the light from the electric bulbs.

"It looks just like snow," she said.

"Sure!" he replied, with a faint smile. "It is snow. Look, I'll show you how to take it."

He divided the powder into halves, took one in the palm of his hand, and snuffed it into his nostrils.

"There!" he exclaimed. "That's the way—it will make you feel like a new woman."

"But what is—it?" she asked. "Won't it hurt me?"

"It'll make you feel bully. Try it."

So she tried it, and it made her "feel bully". She was no longer tired, but deliciously exhilarated.

"Whenever you want any, let me know," he said, as he was leaving the room. "I usually have some handy."

"But I'd like to know what it is," she insisted.

"Aspirin," he replied. "It makes you feel that way when you snuff it up your nose."

After he left, she recovered the little piece of paper from the waste basket where he had thrown it, her curiosity aroused. She found it a rather soiled bit of writing paper with a "C" written in lead pencil upon it.

"'C' " she mused. "Why aspirin with a C?"

She thought she would question Wilson about it.

The next day she felt out of sorts and tired, and at noon she asked him if he had any aspirin with him. He had, and again she felt fine and full of life. That evening she wanted some more, and Crumb gave it to her. The next day she wanted it oftener, and by the time they returned to Hollywood from location she was taking it five or six times a day. It was then that Crumb asked her to come and live with him at the Vista del Paso bungalow; but he did not mention marriage.

He was standing with a little paper of the white powder in his hand, separating half of it for her, and she was waiting impatiently for it.

"Well?" he asked.

"Well, what?"

"Are you coming over to live with me?" he demanded.

"Without being married!" she asked.

She was surprised that the idea no longer seemed horrible. Her eyes and her mind were on the little white powder that the man held in his hand.

Crumb laughed. "Quit your kidding," he said. "You know perfectly well that I can't marry you yet. I have a wife in San Francisco."

She did not know it perfectly well—she did not know it at all; yet it did not seem to matter so very much. A month ago she would have caressed a rattlesnake as willingly as she would have permitted a married man to make love to her; but now she could listen to a plea from one who wished her to come and live with him, without experiencing any numbing sense of outraged decency.

Of course, she had no intention of doing what he asked; but really the matter was of negligible import—the thing in which she was most concerned was the little white powder. She held out her hand for it, but he drew it away.

"Answer me first," he said. "Are you going to be sensible or not?"

"You mean that you won't give it to me if I won't come?" she asked.

"That's precisely what I mean," he replied. "What do you think I am, anyway? Do you know what this bundle of 'C' stands me? Two fifty, and you've been snuffing about three of 'em a day. What kind of a sucker do you think I am?"

Her eyes, still upon the white powder, narrowed.

"I'll come," she whispered. "Give it to me!"

She went to the bungalow with him that day, and she learned where he kept the little white powders, hidden in the bathroom. After dinner she put on her hat and her fur, and took up her vanity case, while Crumb was busy in another room. Then, opening the front door, she called:

"Goodbye!"

"Where are you going?" he demanded.

"Home," she replied.

"No, you're not!" he cried. "You promised to stay here."

"I promised to come," she corrected him. "I never promised to stay, and I never shall until you are divorced and we are married."

"You'll come back," he sneered. "when you want another shot of snow!"

"Oh, I don't know," she replied. "I guess I can buy aspirin at any drug store as well as you."

Crumb laughed aloud.

"You little fool, you!" he cried derisively. "Aspirin! Why, it's cocaine you're snuffing, and you're snuffing about three grains of it a day!"

For an instant a look of horror filled her widened eyes.

"You beast!" she cried. "You unspeakable beast!"

Slamming the door behind her, she almost ran down the narrow walk and disappeared in the shadows of the palm trees that bordered the ill lighted street.

The man did not follow her. He only stood there laughing, for he knew that she would come back. Craftily he had enmeshed her. It had taken months, and never had quarry been more wary or difficult to trap. A single false step earlier in the game would have frightened her away forever; but he had made no false step. He was very proud of himself, was Wilson Crumb, for he was convinced that he had done a very clever bit of work.

Rubbing his hands together, he walked toward the bathroom—he would take a shot of snow; but when he opened the receptacle, he found it empty.

"The little devil!" he ejaculated.

Frantically he rummaged through the medicine cabinet, but in vain. Then he hastened into the living room, seized his hat, and bolted for the street.

Almost immediately he realized the futility of search. He did not know where the girl lived. She had never told him. He did not know it, but she had never told any one. The studio had a post office box number to which it could address communications to Gaza de Lure; the mother addressed the girl by her own name at the house where she had roomed since coming to Hollywood. The woman who rented her the room did not know her screen name. All she knew about her was that she seemed a quiet, refined girl who paid her room rent promptly in advance every week, and who was always home at night, except when on location.

Crumb returned to the bungalow, searched the bathroom twice more, and went to bed. For hours he lay awake, tossing restlessly.

"The little devil!" he muttered, over and over. "Fifty dollars' worth of cocaine—the little devil!"

The next day Gaza was at the studio, ready for work, when Crumb put in a belated appearance. He was nervous and irritable. Almost immediately he called her aside and demanded an accounting; but when they were face to face, and she told him that she was through with him, he realized that her hold upon him was stronger than he has supposed. He could not give her up. He was ready to promise anything, and he would demand nothing in return, only that she would be with him as much as possible. Her nights should be her own —she could go home then. And so the arrangement was consummated, and Gaza de Lure spent the days when she was not working at the bungalow on the Vista del Paso.

Crumb saw that she was cast for small parts that required but little of her time at the studio, yet raised no question at the office as to her salary of fifty dollars a week. Twice the girl asked why he did not star her, and both times he told her that he would—for a price; but the price was one that she would not pay.

As the months passed, Crumb's relations with the source of the supply of their narcotic became so familiar that he could obtain considerable quantities at a reduced rate, and the plan of peddling the drug occurred to him. Gaza was induced to do her share, and so it came about that the better class "hypes" of Hollywood found it both safe and easy to obtain their supplies from the bungalow on the Vista del Paso. Cocaine, heroin, and morphine passed continually through the girl's hands, and she came to know many of the addicts, though she seldom had further intercourse with them than was necessary to the transaction of the business that brought them to the bungalow.

One evening Crumb brought home with him a stranger whom he had known in San Francisco—a man whom he introduced as Allen. From that evening the fortunes of Gaza de Lure improved. Allen had just returned from the Orient as a member of the crew of a freighter, and he had succeeded in smuggling in a considerable quantity of opium. In his efforts to dispose of it he had made the acquaintance of others in the same line of business, and had joined forces with them. His partners could command a more or less steady supply of morphine, and cocaine from Mexico, while Allen undertook to keep up their stock of opium, and to arrange a market for their drugs in Los Angeles.

If Crumb could handle it all, Allen agreed to furnish morphine at fifty dollars an ounce—Gaza to do the actual peddling. The girl agreed on one condition—that half the profits should be hers. After that she had been able to send home more money than ever before, and at the same time to have all the morphine she wanted at a low price. She began to put money in the bank, made a first payment on a small orchard about a hundred miles from Los Angeles, and sent for her mother.

The day before you called on her in the "art" bungalow at 1421 Vista del Paso she had put her mother on a train bound for her new home, with the promise that the daughter would visit her "as soon as we finish this picture." It had required all the girl's remaining will power to hide her shame from those eager mother eyes; but she had managed to do it, though it had left her almost a wreck by the time the train pulled out of the station.

To Crumb she had said nothing about her mother. This was a part of her life that was too sacred to be revealed to the man whom she now loathed even as she loathed the filthy habit he had tricked her into; but she could no more give up the one than the other.

CHAPTER VI

It was May. The rainy season was definitely over. A few April showers had concluded it. The Ganado hills showed their most brilliant greens. The March pigs were almost ready to wean. White-faced calves and black colts and gray colts surveyed this beautiful world through soft, dark eyes, and were filled with the joy of living as they ran beside their gentle mothers. A stallion neighed from the stable corral, and from the ridge behind Jackknife Canyon the Emperor of Ganado answered him.

A girl and a man sat in the soft grass beneath the shade of alive oak upon the edge of a low bluff in the pasture where the brood mares grazed with their colts. Their horses were tied to another tree near by. The girl held a bunch of yellow violets in her hand, and gazed dreamily down the broad canyon toward the valley. The man sat a little behind her and gazed at the girl. For a long time neither spoke.

"You cannot be persuaded to give it up, Grace?" he asked at last. She shook her head.

"I shall never be happy until I had tried it," she replied.

"Of course," he said, "I know how you feel about it. I feel the same way. I want to get away—away from the deadly stagnation and sameness of this life; but I am going to try to stick it out for father's sake, and I wish that you loved me enough to stick it out for mine. I believe that together we could get enough happiness out of life here to make up for what we are denied of real living, such as only a big city can offer. Then, when father is gone, we could go and live in the city—in any city that we wanted to live in—Los Angeles, Chicago, New York, London, Paris—anywhere. "

"I know," she said, and they were silent again for a time. "You are a good son, Custer," she said presently. "I wouldn't have you any different. I am not so good a daughter. Mother does not want me to go. It is going to make her very unhappy, and yet I am going. The man who loves me does not want me to go. It is going to make him very unhappy, and yet I am going. It seems very selfish; but oh, Custer, I cannot help but feel I am right! It seems to me that I have a duty to perform, and that this is the only way I can perform it. Perhaps I am not only silly, but sometimes I feel that I am called by a higher power to give myself for a little time to the world, that the world may be happier and, I hope, a little better. You know I have always felt that the stage was one of the greatest powers for good in all the world, and now I believe that some day the screen will be an even greater power for good. It is with the conviction that I may help toward this end that I am so eager to go. You will be very glad and very happy when I come back, that I did not listen to your arguments."

"I hope you are right, Grace." Custer Pennington said.

On a rustic seat beneath the new leaves of an umbrella tree a girl and a boy sat beside the upper lily pond on the south side of the hill below the ranch house. The girl held a spray of Japanese quince blossoms in her hand, and gazed dreamily at the water splashing lazily over the rocks into the pond. The boy sat beside her and gazed at the girl. For a long time neither spoke.

"Won't you please say yes?" whispered the boy presently.

"How perfectly, terribly silly you are!" she replied.

"I am not silly," he said. "I am twenty, and you are almost eighteen. It's time that we were marrying and settling down."

"On what?" she demanded.

"Well, we won't need much at first. We can live at home with mother," he explained, "until I sell a few stories."

"How perfectly gorgeristic!" she cried.

"Don't make fun of me! You wouldn't if you loved me," he pouted.

"I do love you silly! But whatever in the world put the dapper little idea into your head that I wanted to be supported by my mother-in-law?"

"Aw, come, now, you needn't get mad at me. I was only fooling; but wouldn't it be great, Ev? We could always be together then, and I could write and you could—could—"

"Wash dishes," she suggested. The light died from his eyes.

"I'm sorry I'm poor," he said. "I didn't think you cared about that, though."

She laid a brown hand gently over his.

"You know I don't care," she said. "I am a catty old thing. I'd just love it if we had a little place all our very own just a teeny, weeny bungalow. I'd help you with your work, and keep hens, and have a little garden with onions and radishes and everything, and we wouldn't have to buy anything from the grocery store, and a bank account, and one sow; and when we drove into the city people would say, 'There goes Guy Thackeray Evans, the famous author, but I wonder where his wife got that hat!' "

"Oh Ev!" he cried laughing. "You never can be serious more than two seconds can you?"

"Why should I be?" she inquired. "And anyway, I was. It really would be elegantiferous if we had a little place of our own; but my husband has got to be able to support me, Guy. He'd lose his self-respect if he didn't; and then, if he lost his, how could I respect him? You've got to have respect on both sides, or you can't have love and happiness."

His face grew stern with determination.

"I'll get the money," he said; but he did not look at her. "But now that Grace is going away, mother will be all alone if I leave, too. Couldn't we live with her for a while?"

"Papa and mama have always said that it was the worst thing a young married couple could do," she replied. "We could live near her, and see her every day; but I don't think we should all live together. Really though, do you think Grace is going? It seems just too awful."

"I am afraid she is," he replied sadly. "Mother is all broken up about it; but she tries not to let Grace know."

"I can't understand it," said the girl. "It seems to me a selfish thing to do, and yet Grace has always been so sweet and generous. No matter how much I wanted to go, I don't believe I could bring myself to do it, knowing how terribly it would hurt papa. Just think, Guy—it is the first break, except for the short time we were away at school, since we have been born. We have all lived here always, it seems, your family and mine, like one big family; but after Grace goes it will be the beginning of the end. It will never be the same again."

There was a note of seriousness and sadness in her voice that sounded not at all like Eva Pennington. The boy shook his head.

"It is too bad," he said; "but Grace is so sure she is right—so positive that she has a great future before her, and that we shall all be so proud of her—that sometimes I am convinced myself."

The girl rose.

"Come on!" she said. "Let's have a look at the pools—it isn't a perfect day unless I've seen fish in every pool. Do you remember how we used to watch and watch and watch for the fish in the lower pools, and run as fast as we could to be the first up to the house to tell if we saw them, and how many?"

They walked on in silence along the winding pathways among the flower-bordered pools, to stop at last beside the lower one. This had originally been a shallow wading pool for the children when they were small, but it was now given over to water hyacinth and brilliant fantails.

"There!" said the girl, presently. "I have seen fish in each pool."

"And you can go to bed with a clear conscience tonight," he laughed.

To the west of the lower pool there were no trees to obstruct their view of the hills that rolled down from the mountains to form the western wall of the canyon in which the ranch buildings and cultivated fields lay. As the two stood there, hand in hand, the boy's eyes wandered lovingly over the soft, undulating lines of these lower hills, with their parklike beauty of greensward dotted with wild walnut trees. As he looked he saw, for a brief moment, the figure of a man on horseback passing over the hollow of a saddle before disappearing upon the southern side.

Small though the distant figure was, and visible but for a moment, the boy recognized the military carriage of the rider. He glanced quickly at the girl to note if she had seen, but it was evident that she had not.

"Well, Ev," he said, "l guess I'll be toddling."

"So early?" she demanded.

"You see I've got to get busy, if I'm going to get the price of that teeny, weeny bungalow," he explained.

A moment later he swung into the saddle, and with a wave of his hand cantered off up the canyon.

"Now what," said the girl to herself, "is he going up there for? He can't make any money back there in the hills. He ought to be headed straight for home and his typewriter!"

CHAPTER VII

Across the rustic bridge, and once behind the sycamores at the lower end of the cow pasture, Guy Evans let his horse out into a rapid gallop. A few minutes later he overtook a horseman who was moving at a slow walk farther up the canyon. At the sound of the pounding hoof-beats behind him, the latter turned in his saddle, reined about and stopped. The boy rode up and drew in his blowing mount beside the other.

"Hello, Allen!" he said.

The man nodded.

"What's eatin' you?" he inquired.

"I've been thinking over that proposition of yours," explained Evans.

"Yes?"

"Yes, I've been thinking maybe I might swing it; but are you sure it's safe. How do I know you won't double-cross me?"

"You don't know," replied the other. "All you know is that I got enough on you to send you to San Quentin. You wouldn't get nothin' worse if you handled the rest of it, an' you stand to clean up between twelve and fifteen thousand bucks on the deal. You needn't worry about me double-crossin' you. What good would it do me? I ain't got nothin' against you, kid. If you don't double-cross me I won't double-cross you; but look out for that cracker-fed dude your sister's goin' to hitch to. If he ever butts in on this I'll croak him an' send you to San Quentin, if I swing for it. Do you get me?"

Evans nodded.

"I'll go in on it," he said, "because I need the money; but don't you bother Custer Pennington—get that straight. I'd go to San Quentin and I'd swing myself before I'd stand for that. Another thing, and then we'll drop that line of chatter—you couldn't send me to San Quentin or anywhere else. I bought a few bottles of hooch from you, and there isn't any judge or jury going to send me to San Quentin for that."

"You don't know what you done," said Allen, with a grin. "There's a thousand cases of bonded whiskey hid back there in the hills, an' you engineered the whole deal at this end. Maybe you didn't have nothin' to do with stealin' it from a government bonded warehouse in New York; but you must a' knowed all about it, an' it was you that hired me and the other three to smuggle it off the ship and into the hills."

Evans was staring at the man in wide-eyed incredulity.

"How do you get that way?" he asked derisively.

"They's four of us to swear to it," said Allen; "an' how many you got to swear you didn't do it?"

"Why, it's a rotten frame-up!" exclaimed Evans.

"Sure it's a frame-up," agreed Allen; "but we won't use it if you behave yourself properly."

Evans looked at the man for a long minute—dislike and contempt unconcealed upon his face.

"I guess," he said presently, "that I don't need any twelve thousand dollars that bad, Allen. We'll call this thing off, as far as I am concerned. I'm through, right now. Goodbye!"

He wheeled his horse to ride away.

"Hold on there, young feller!" said Allen. "Not so quick! You may think you're through, but you're not. We need you, and, anyway, you know too damned much for your health. You're goin' through with this. We got some other junk up there that there's more profit in than what there is in booze, and it's easier to handle. We know where to get rid of it; but the booze we can't handle as easy as you can, and so you're goin' to handle it."

"Who says I am?"

"I do," returned Allen, with an ugly snarl. "You'll handle it, or I'll do just what I said I'd do, and I'll do it pronto. How'd you like your mother and that Pennington girl to hear all I'd have to say?"

The boy sat with scowling, thoughtful brows for a long minute. From beneath a live oak, on the summit of a low bluff, a man discovered them. He had been sitting there talking with a girl. Suddenly he looked up.

"Why, there's Guy," he said. "Who's that with—why, it's that fellow Allen! What's he doing up here?" He rose to his feet. "You stay here a minute, Grace, I'm going down to see what that fellow wants. I can't understand Guy."

He untied the Apache and mounted, while below, just beyond the pasture fence, the boy turned sullenly toward Allen.

"I'll go through with it this once," he said. "You'll bring it down on burros at night?"

The other nodded affirmatively.

"Where do you want it?" he asked.

"Bring it to the west side of the old hay barn—the one that stands on our west line. When will you come?"

"Today's Tuesday. We'll bring the first lot Friday night, about twelve o'clock; and after that every Friday the same time. You be ready to settle every Friday for what you've sold during the week—sabe?"

"Yes," replied Evans. "That's all, then"; and he turned and rode back toward the rancho.

Allen was continuing on his way toward the hills when his attention was again attracted by the sound of hoofbeats. Looking to his left, he saw a horseman approaching from inside the pasture. He recognized both horse and rider at once, but kept sullenly on his way.

Pennington rode up to the opposite side of the fence along which ran the trail that Allen followed.

"What are you doing here, Allen?" he asked in a not unkindly tone.

"Mindin' my own business, like you better," retorted the ex-stableman.

"You have no business back here on Ganado," said Pennington. "You'll have to get off the property."

"The hell I will!" exclaimed Allen.

At the same time he made a quick movement with his right hand but Pennington made a quicker.

"That kind of stuff don't go here, Allen," said the younger man, covering the other with a forty-five. "Now turn around and get off the place, and don't come on it again. I don't want any trouble with you."

Without a word, Allen reined his horse about and rode down the canyon; but there was murder in his heart. Pennington watched him until he was out of revolver range, and then turned and rode back to Grace Evans.

CHAPTER VIII

Beneath the cool shadows of the north porch the master of Ganado, booted and spurred, rested after a long ride in the hot sun, sipping a long, cool glass of peach brandy and orange juice, and talking to his wife.

She knew the dream that her husband had built, and that with it he had purposely blinded his eyes and dulled his ears to the truth which the mother heart would have been glad to deny, but could not. Some day one of the children would go away, and then the other. It was only right and just that it should be so, for as they two had built their own home and their own lives and their little family circle, so their children must do even as they.

It was going to be hard on them both, much harder on the father, because of that dream that had become an obsession. Mrs. Pennington feared that it might break his spirit, for it would leave him nothing to plan for and hope for as he had planned and hoped for during the twenty-two years that they had spent upon Ganado.

Now that Grace was going to the city, how could they hope to keep their boy content upon the ranch? She knew he loved the old place, but he was entitled to see the world and to make his own place in it—not merely to slide spinelessly into the niche that another had prepared for him.

"I am worried about the boy," she said presently.

"How? In what way?" he asked.

"He will be very blue and lonely after Grace goes," she said.

"Damned foolishness, that's what it is!" he blustered. "An actress! What does she know about acting?"

"Have you ever thought that some day our own children may want to go?" she asked.

"I won't think about it!" he exploded.

"I hope you won't have to," she said; "but it's going to be pretty hard on the boy after Grace goes."

"Do you think he'll want to go?" the colonel asked. His voice sounded suddenly strange and pleading, and there was a suggestion of pain and fear in his eyes that she had never seen there before in all the years that she had known him. "Do you think he'll want to go?" he repeated in a voice that no longer sounded like his own.

"Stranger things have happened," she replied, forcing a smile, "than a young man wanting to go out into the world and win his spurs!"

"Let's not talk about it, Julia," the colonel said presently. "You are right, but I don't want to think about it. When it comes will be time enough to meet it. If my boy wants to go, he shall go—and he shall never know how deeply his father is hurt!"

"There they are now," said Mrs. Pennington. "I hear them in the patio. Children!" she called. "Here we are on the north porch!"

They came through the house together, brother and sister, their arms about each other.

"Cus says I am too young to get married," exclaimed the girl.

"Married!" ejaculated the colonel. "You and Guy talking of getting married? What are you going to live on, child?"

"On the hill back there."

She jerked her thumb in a direction that was broadly south by west.

"That will give them two things to live on," suggested the boy, grinning.

"What do you mean—two things?" demanded the girl.

"The hill and father," her brother replied, dodging.

She pursued him, and he ran behind his mother's chair; but at last she caught him, and, seizing his collar, pretended to chastise him, until he picked her up bodily from the floor and kissed her.

"Pity the poor goof she ensnares!" pleaded Custer, addressing his parents. "He will have three avenues of escape—being beaten to death, starved to death, or talked to death."

Eva clapped a hand over his mouth.

"Now listen to me," she cried. "Guy and I are going to build a teeny, weeny bungalow on that hill, all by ourselves, with a white tile splash board in the kitchen, and one of those broom closets that turn into an ironing board, and a very low, overhanging roof, almost flat, and a shower, and a great big living room where we can take up the rugs and dance, and a spiffy little garden in the back yard, and chickens, and Chinese rugs, and he is going to have a study all to himself where he writes his stories, an —"

At last she had to stop and join in the laughter.

"I think you are all mean," she added. "You always laugh at me!"

"With you, little jabberer," corrected the colonel; "for you were made to be laughed with and kissed."

"Then kiss me," she exclaimed, and sprang into his lap, at the imminent risk of deluging them both with "elixir"—a risk which the colonel, through long experience of this little daughter of his, was able to minimize by holding the glass at arm's length as she dived for him.

"And when are you going to be married?" he asked.

"Oh, not for ages and ages!" she cried.

"But are you and Guy engaged?"

"Of course not!"

"Then why in the world all this talk about getting married?" he inquired, his eyes twinkling.

"Well, can't I talk?" she demanded.

"Talk? I'll say she can!" exclaimed her brother.

CHAPTER IX

Two weeks later Grace Evans left for Hollywood and fame. She would permit no one to accompany her, saying that she wanted to feel that the moment she left home she had made her own way, unassisted, toward her goal.

Hers was the selfish egotism that is often to be found in otherwise generous natures. She had never learned the sweetness and beauty of sharing—of sharing her ambitions, her successes, and her failures, too, with those who loved her. If she won to fame, the glory would be hers; nor did it once occur to her that she might have shared that pride and pleasure with others by accepting their help and advice. If she failed, they would not have even the sad sweetness of sharing her disappointment.

Over two homes there hovered that evening a pall of gloom that no effort seemed able to dispel. In the ranch house on Ganado they made a brave effort at cheerfulness on Custer Pennington's account. They did not dance that evening, as was their custom, nor could they find pleasure in the printed page which they tried to read. Bridge proved equally impossible.

Finally Custer rose, announcing that he was going to bed. Kissing them all good night, as had been the custom since childhood, he went to his room, and tears came to the mother's eyes as she noted the droop in the broad shoulders as he walked from the room.

The girl came then and knelt beside her, taking the older woman's hand in hers and caressing it.

"I feel so sorry for Cus," she said. "I believe that none of us realize how hard he is taking this. He told me yesterday that it was going to be just the same as if Grace was dead, for he knew she would never be satisfied here again, whether she succeeded or failed. I think he has definitely given up all hope of their being married."

"Oh, no, dear, I am sure he is wrong," said her mother. "The engagement has not been broken. In fact Grace told me only a few days ago that she hoped her success would come quickly, so that she and Custer might be married the sooner. The dear girl wants us to be proud of our new daughter."

"My God!" ejaculated the colonel, throwing his book down and rising to pace the floor. "Proud of her! Weren't we already proud of her? Will being an actress make her any dearer to us? Of all the damn fool ideas!"

"Custer! Custer! You mustn't swear so before Eva," reproved Mrs. Pennington.

"Swear?" he demanded. "Who in the hell is swearing?"

A merry peal of laughter broke from the girl, nor could her mother refrain from smiling.

"It isn't swearing when popsy says it," cried the girl. "My gracious, I've heard it all my life, and you always say the same thing to him, as if I'd never heard a single little cuss word. Anyway, I'm going to bed now, popsy, so that you won't contaminate me. According to momsy's theory she should curse like a pirate by this time, after twenty-five years of it!"

She kissed them, leaving them alone in the little family sitting room.

"I hope the boy won't take it too hard," said the colonel after a silence.

"I am afraid he has been drinking a little too much lately," said the mother. "I only hope his loneliness for Grace won't encourage it."

"I hadn't noticed it," said the colonel.

"He never shows it much," she replied. "An outsider would not know that he had been drinking at all when I can see that he has had more than he should."

"Don't worry about that, dear," said the colonel. "A Pennington never drinks more than a gentleman should. His father and his grandsires, on both sides, always drank, but there has never been a drunkard in either family. I wouldn't give two cents for him if he couldn't take a man's drink like a man; but he'll never go too far. My boy couldn't."

The pride and affection in the words brought the tears to the mother's eyes. She wondered if there had ever been father and son like these before— each with such implicit confidence in the honor, the integrity, and the manly strength of the other. His boy couldn't go wrong!

Custer Pennington entered his room, lighted a reading lamp beside a deep, wide-armed chair, selected a book from a rack, and settled himself comfortably for an hour of pleasure and inspiration. But he did not open the book. Instead, he sat staring blindly at the opposite wall.

She would never come back and why should she? In the city, in that new life, she would meet men of the world—men of broader culture than his, men of wealth—and she would be sought after. They would have more to offer her than he, and sooner or later she would realize it. He could not expect to hold her.

Custer laid aside his book.

"What's the use?" he asked himself.

Rising, he went to the closet and brought out a bottle. He had not intended drinking. On the contrary, he had determined very definitely not to drink that night; but again he asked himself the old question which, under certain circumstances of life and certain conditions of seeming hopelessness, appears unanswerable:

"What is the use?"

It is a foolish question, a meaningless question, a dangerous question. What is the use of what? Of combating fate—of declining to do the thing we ought not to do—of doing the thing we should do? It is not even a satisfactory means of self-justification; but amid the ruins of his dreams it was sufficient excuse for Custer Pennington's surrender to the craving of an appetite which was daily becoming stronger.

The next morning he did not ride before breakfast with the other members of the family nor in fact, did he breakfast until long after they.

On the evening of the day of Grace's departure Mrs. Evans retired early, complaining of a headache. Guy Evans sought to interest himself in various magazines, but he was restless and too ill at ease to remain long absorbed. At frequent intervals he consulted his watch, and as the evening wore on he made numerous trips to his room, where he had recourse to a bottle like the one with which Custer Pennington was similarly engaged.

It was Friday—the second Friday since Guy had entered into an agreement with Allen; and as midnight approached his nervousness increased.

Time and again, during that long evening, he mentally reiterated his determination that once this venture was concluded, he would never embark upon another of a similar nature. The several thousand dollars which it would net him would make it possible for him to marry Eva and settle down to a serious and uninterrupted effort at writing—the one vocation for which he believed himself best fitted by inclination and preparation; but never again, he assured himself repeatedly, would he allow himself to be cajoled or threatened into such an agreement.

As he sat waiting for the arrival of the second consignment, he pictured the little cavalcade winding downward along hidden trails through the chaparral of dark, mountain ravines. His nervousness increased as he realized the risk of discovery some time during the six months that it would take to move the contraband to the edge of the valley in this way—thirty-six cases at a time, packed out on six burros.

He had little fear of the failure of his plan for hiding the liquor in the old hay barn and moving it out again the following day. For three years there had been stored in one end of the barn some fifty tons of baled melilotus. It had been sown as a cover crop by a former foreman, and allowed to grow to such proportions as to render the plowing of it under a practical impossibility. As hay it was in little or no demand, but there was a possibility of a hay shortage that year. It was against this possibility that Evans had had it baled and stored away in the barn, where it had lain ever since, awaiting an offer that would at least cover the cost of growing, harvesting, and baling. A hard day's work had so re-arranged the bales as to form a hidden chamber in the center of the pile, ingress to which could readily be had by removing a couple of bales near the floor.

A little after eleven o'clock Guy left the house and made his way to the barn, where he paced nervously to and fro in the dark interior. He hoped that the men would come early and get the thing over, for it was this part of the operation that seemed most fraught with danger.

The whiskey was in Guy's possession for less than twelve hours a week; but during those twelve hours he earned the commission of a dollar a bottle that Allen allowed him, for his great fear was that sooner or later some one would discover and follow the six burros as they came down to the barn. There were often campers in the hills. During the deer season, if they did not have it all removed by that time, they would be almost certain of discovery, since every courageous ribbon-counter clerk in Los Angeles hied valiantly to the mountains with a high-powered rifle, to track the ferocious deer to its lair.

At a quarter past twelve Evans heard the sounds for which he had been so expectantly waiting. He opened a small door in the end of the hay barn, through which there filed in silence six burdened burros, led by one swarthy Mexican and followed by another. Quietly the men unpacked the burros and stored the thirty-six cases in the chamber beneath the hay. Inside this same chamber, by the light of a flash lamp, Evans counted out to one of them the proceeds from the sale of the previous week. The whole transaction consumed less than half an hour, and was carried on with the exchange of less than a dozen words. As silently as they had come the men departed, with their burros, into the darkness toward the hills, and young Evans made his way to his room and to bed.

CHAPTER X

As the weeks passed, the routine of ranch life weighed more and more heavily on Custer Pennington. The dull monotony of it took the zest from the things that he had formerly regarded as the pleasures of existence. The buoyant Apache no longer had power to thrill. The long rides were but obnoxious duties to be performed. The hills had lost their beauty.

The frequent letters that came from Grace during her first days in Hollywood had breathed a spirit of hopefulness and enthusiasm that might have proven contagious, but for the fact that he saw in her success a longer and probably a permanent separation. If she should be speedily discouraged she might return to the foothills and put the idea of a career forever from her mind; but if she received even the slightest encouragement, Custer was confident that nothing could wean her from her ambition. He was the more sure of this because in his own mind he could picture no inducement sufficiently powerful to attract any one to return to the humdrum existence of the ranch. Better be a failure in the midst of life, he put it to himself, than a success in the unpeopled spaces of its outer edge.

Ensuing weeks brought fewer letters, and there was less of enthusiasm, though hope was still unquenched. She had not yet met the right people, Grace said, and there was a general depression in the entire picture industry.

The little gatherings of the neighbors at Ganado continued. Other young people of the valley and the foothills came and danced, or swam, or played tennis. Their elders came, too, equally enjoying the hospitality of the Penningtons; and among these was the new owner of the little orchard beyond the Evans ranch.

As she came oftener, and came to know the Penningtons better, she depended more and more on the colonel for advice in matters pertaining to her orchard and her finances. Of personal matters she never spoke. They knew that she had a daughter living in Los Angeles; but of the girl they knew nothing, for deep in the heart of Mrs. George Burke, who had been born Charity Cooper, was a strain of Puritanism that could not look with aught but horror upon the stage and its naughty little sister, the screen—though in her letters to that loved daughter there was no suggestion of the pain that the fond heart held because of the career the girl had chosen.

While life upon Ganado took its peaceful way, outwardly unruffled, the girl whose image was in the hearts of them all strove valiantly in the face of recurring disappointment toward the high goal upon which her eyes were set.

She was interviewing, for the dozenth time, the casting director of the K. K. S. Studio, who had come to know her by sight, and perhaps to feel a little compassion for her—though there are those who will tell you that casting directors, having no hearts, can never experience so human an emotion as compassion.

"I'm sorry, Miss Evans," he said; "but I haven't a thing for you to-day." As she turned away, he raised his hand. "Wait!" he said. "Mr. Crumb is casting his new picture himself. He's out on the lot now. Go out and see him —he might be able to use you."

A few minutes later she found the man she sought. She had never seen Wilson Crumb before, and her first impression was a pleasant one, for he was courteous and affable. She told him that she had been to the casting director, and that he had said that Mr. Crumb might be able to use her. As she spoke, the man watched her intently, his eyes running quickly over her figure without suggesting offense.

"What experience have you had?" he asked.

"Just a few times as an extra," she replied.

He shook his head.

"I am afraid I can't use you," he said; "unless"—he hesitated —"unless you would care to work in the semi-nude, which would necessitate making a test—in the nude."

"Is that absolutely essential?" she asked.

"Quite so," he replied.

Still she hesitated. Her chance! If she let it pass, she might as well pack up and return home. What a little thing to do, after all, when one really considered it! It was purely professional. There would be nothing personal in it, if she could only succeed in overcoming her self-consciousness; but could she do it?

Two hours later Grace Evans, left the K.K.S. lot. She was to start work on the morrow at fifty dollars a week for the full period of the picture. Wilson Crumb had told her that she had a wonderful future, and that she was fortunate to have fallen in with a director who could make a great star of her. As she went, she left behind all her self-respect and part of her natural modesty.

Wilson Crumb, watching her go, rubbed the ball of his right thumb to and fro across the back of his left hand, and smiled.

The Apache danced along the wagon trail that led back into the hills. He tugged at the bit and tossed his head impatiently, flecking his rider's shirt with foam. He lifted his feet high and twisted and wriggled like an eel. He wanted to be off, and he wondered what had come over his old pal that there was no more swift gay gallops, and that washes were crossed sedately by way of their gravelly bottoms, instead of being taken with a flying leap.

It was Friday. From the hill beyond Jackknife a man had watched through binoculars his every move. Three other men had been waiting below the watcher along the new-made trail.

"It was young Pennington," he said. The speaker was Allen. "I was thinking that it would be a fool trick to kill him, unless we have to. I have a better scheme. Listen—if he ever learns anything that he shouldn't know, this is what you are to do, if I am away."

Very carefully and in great detail he elaborated his plan. "Do you understand?" he asked.

They did, and they grinned.

The following night, after the Penningtons had dined, a ranch hand came up from Mrs. Burke's to tell them that their new neighbor was quite ill, and that the woman who did her housework wanted Mrs. Pennington to come down at once as she was worried about her mistress.

"We will be right down," said Colonel Pennington.

They found Mrs. Burke breathing with difficulty, and the colonel immediately telephoned for a local doctor. After the physician had examined her, he came to them in the living room.

"You had better send for Jones, of Los Angeles," he said. "It is her heart. I can do nothing. I doubt if he can; but he is a specialist. And," he added, "if she has any near relatives, I think I should notify them— at once."

The housekeeper had joined them, and was wiping tears from her face with her apron.

"She has a daughter in Los Angeles," said the colonel; "but we do not know her address."

"She wrote to her to-day, just before this spell," said the housekeeper. "The letter hasn't been mailed yet—here it is."

She picked it up from the center table and handed it to the colonel.

"Miss Shannon Burke, 1580 Panizo Circle, Hollywood," he read. "I will take the responsibility of wiring both Miss Burke and Dr. Jones. Can you get a good nurse locally?"

The doctor could, and so it was arranged.

CHAPTER XI

Gaza de Lure was sitting at the piano when Crumb arrived at the bungalow at 1421 Vista del Paso at a little after six in the evening of the last Saturday in July. The smoke from a half burned cigarette lying on the ebony case was rising in a thin, indolent column above the masses of her black hair. Her fingers idled through a dreamy waltz. Crumb gave her a surly nod as he closed the door behind him. He was tired and cross after a hard day at the studio. The girl, knowing that he would be all right presently, merely returned his nod and continued playing. He went immediately to his room, and a moment later she heard him enter the bathroom through another doorway.

Half an hour later he emerged, shaved, spruce, and smiling. A tiny powder had effected a transformation, just as she had known that it would. He came and leaned across the piano, close to her. She was very beautiful. It seemed to the man that she grew more beautiful and more desirable each day. The fact that she had been unattainable had fed the fires of his desire, transforming infatuation into as near a thing to love as a man of his type can ever feel.

"Well, little girl!" he cried gaily. "I have good news for you."

She smiled a crooked little smile, and shook her head.

"The only good news that I can think of would be that the government had established a comfortable home for superannuated hop-heads, where they would be furnished, without cost, with all the snow they could use."

The effects of her last shot were wearing off. He laughed good-naturedly.

"Really," he insisted; "on the level, I've got the best news you've heard in moons."

"Well?" she asked wearily.

"Old Battle-Axe has got her divorce," he announced, referring thus affectionately to his wife.

"Well," said the girl, "that's good news—for her—if it's true." Crumb frowned.

"It's good news for you," he said. "It means that I can marry you now."

The girl leaned back on the piano bench and laughed aloud. It was not a pleasant laugh. She laughed until the tears rolled down her cheeks.

"What is there funny about that?" growled the man. "It would mean a lot to you—respectability, for one thing, and success, for another. The day you become Mrs. Wilson Crumb I'll star you in the greatest picture that was ever made."

"Respectability!" she sneered. "Your name would make me respectable, would it? It would be the insult added to all the injury you have done me. And as for starring—poof!" She snapped her fingers. "I have but one ambition, thanks to you, you dirty hound, and that is snow!" She leaned toward him, her two clenched fists almost shaking in his face. "Give me all the snow I need," she cried, "and the rest of them may have their fame and their laurels!"

"Oh, very well," he said. "If you feel that way about it, all right; but" —he turned suddenly upon her—"you'll have to get out of here and stay out—do you understand? From this day on you can only enter this house as Mrs. Wilson Crumb, and you can rustle your own dope if you don't come back— understand?"

She looked at him through narrowed lids. She reminded him of a tigress about to spring, and he backed away.

"Listen to me," she commanded in slow, level tones. "In the first place, you're lying to me about your wife getting her divorce. I'd have guessed as much if I hadn't known, for a hop-head can't tell the truth; but I do know. You got a letter from your attorney to-day telling you that your wife still insists not only that she will never divorce you, but that she will never allow you a divorce."

"You mean to say that you opened one of my letters?" he demanded angrily.

"Sure I opened it! I open 'em all—I steam 'em open. What do you expect," she almost screamed, "from the thing you have made of me? Do you expect honor and self-respect, or any other virtue in a hype?"

"You can get out of here!" he cried. "You get out now—this minute!"

She rose from the bench and came and stood quite close to him.

"You'll see that I get all the snow I want, if I go?" she asked. He laughed nastily.

"You don't ever get another bindle," he replied.

"Wait!" she admonished. "I wasn't through with what I started to say a minute ago. You've been hitting it long enough, Wilson, to know what one of our kind will do to get it. You know that either you or I would sacrifice soul and body if there was no other way. We would lie, or steal, or— murder! Do you get that, Wilson—murder? There is just one thing I won't do, but that one thing is not murder, Wilson. Listen!" She lifted her face close to his and looked him straight in the eyes. "If you ever try to take it away from me, or keep it from me, Wilson, I shall kill you."

Her tone was cold and unemotional, and because of that, perhaps, the threat seemed very real. The man paled.

"Aw, come!" he cried. "What's the use of our scrapping? I was only kidding, anyway. Run along and take a shot— it'll make you feel better."

"Yes," she said, "I need one; but don't get it into your head that I was kidding. I wasn't. I'd just as lief kill you as not— the only trouble is that killing's too damned good for you, Wilson!"

She walked toward the bathroom door.

"Oh, by the way," she said, pausing. "Allen called up this afternoon. He's in town, and will be up after dinner. He wants his money."

She entered the bathroom and closed the door. Crumb lighted another cigarette and threw himself into an easy chair, where he sat scowling at a temple dog on a Chinese rug.

A moment later Gaza joined Crumb in the little dining room. They both smoked throughout the meal, which they scarcely ever tasted. The girl was vivacious and apparently happy. She seemed to have forgotten the recent scene in the living room. She asked questions about the new picture.

"We're going to commence shooting Monday," he told her. Momentarily he waxed almost enthusiastic. "I'm going to have trouble with that boob author, though," he said. "If they'd kick him off the lot, and give me a little more money, I'd make 'em the greatest picture ever screened!" Then he relapsed into brooding silence.

"What's the matter?" she asked. "Worrying about Allen?"

"Not exactly," he said. "I'll stall him off again."

"He isn't going to be easy to stall this time," she observed, "if I gathered the correct idea from his line of talk over the phone to-day. I can't see what you've done with all the coin, Wilson."

"You got yours, didn't you?" he growled.

"Sure I got mine," she answered, "and it's nothing to me what you did with Allen's share; but I'm here to tell you that you've pulled a boner if you've double-crossed him. I'm not much of a character reader, as proved by my erstwhile belief that you were a high-minded gentleman; but it strikes me the veriest boob could see that that man Allen is a bad actor. You'd better look out for him."

"I ain't afraid of him," blustered Crumb.

"No, of course you're not," she agreed sarcastically. "You're a regular little lion-hearted Reginald, Wilson—that's what you are!"

The doorbell rang. "There he is now," said the girl.

Crumb paled.

"What makes you think he's a bad man?" he asked.

"Look at his face—look at his eyes," she admonished. "Hard? He's got a face like a brick-bat."

They rose from the table and entered the living room as the Japanese opened the front door. The caller was Slick Allen. Crumb rushed forward and greeted him effusively.

"Hello, old man!" he cried. "I'm mighty glad to see you. Miss de Lure told me that you had phoned. Can't tell you how delighted I am!"

Allen nodded to the girl, tossed his cap upon a bench near the door, and crossed to the center of the room.

"Won't you sit down, Mr. Allen?" she suggested.

"I ain't got much time," he said, lowering himself into a chair. "I come up here, Crumb, to get some money." His cold, fishy eyes looked straight into Crumb's. "I come to get all the money there is comin' to me. It's a trifle over ten thousand dollars, as I figure it.

"Yes," said Crumb; "that's about it."

"An' I don't want no stallin' this time, either," concluded Allen. "Stalling!" exclaimed Crumb in a hurt tone. "Who's been stalling?"

"You have."

"Oh, my dear man!" cried Crumb deprecatingly. "You know that in matters of this kind one must be circumspect. There were reasons in the past why it would have been unsafe to transfer so large an amount to you. It might easily have been traced. I was being watched— a fellow even shadowed me to the teller's window in my bank one day. You see how it is? Neither of us can take chances."

"That's all right, too," said Allen; "but I've been taking chances right along, and I ain't been taking them for my health. I been taking them for the coin, and I want that coin—I want it pronto!"

"You can most certainly have it," said Crumb.

"All right!" replied Allen, extending a palm. "Fork it over."

"My dear fellow you don't think that I have it here, do you?" demanded Crumb. "You don't think I keep such an amount as that in my home, I hope!"

"Where is it?"

"In the bank, of course."

"Gimme a check."

"You must be crazy! Suppose either of us was suspected; that check would link up us fine. It would be as bad for you as for me. Nothing doing! I'll get the cash when the bank opens on Monday. That's the very best I can do. If you'd written and let me know you were coming, I could have had it for you. "

Allen eyed him for a long minute.

"Very well," he said, at last. "I'll wait till noon Monday." Crumb breathed an inward sigh of profound relief.

"If you're at the bank Monday morning, at half past ten, you'll get the money," he said. "How's the other stuff going? Sorry I couldn't handle that, but it's too bulky."

"The hooch? It's goin' fine," replied Allen. "Got a young high-blood at the edge of the valley handlin' it—fellow by the name of Evans. He moves thirty-six cases a week. The kid's got a good head on him— worked the whole scheme out himself. Sells the whole batch every week, for cash, to a guy with a big truck. They cover it with hay, and this guy hauls it right into the city in broad daylight, unloads it in a warehouse he's rented, slips each case into a carton labeled somebody or other's soap, and delivers it a case at a time to a bunch of drug stores. This second guy used to be a drug salesman, and he's personally acquainted with every grafter in the business."

As he talked, Allen had been studying the girl's face. She had noticed it before; but she was used to having men stare at her, and thought little of it. Finally he addressed her.

"Do you know, Miss de Lure," he said, "there's something mighty familiar about your face? I noticed it the first time I came here, and I been studyin' over it since. It seems like I'd known you somewhere else, or some one you look a lot like; but I can't quite get it straight in my head. I can't make out where it was, or when, or if it was you or some one else. I'll get it some day, though."

"I don't know," she replied. "I'm sure I never saw you before you came here with Mr. Crumb the first time."

"Well, I don't know, either," replied Allen, scratching his head; "but it's mighty funny." He arose. "I'll be goin'," he said. "See you Monday at the bank—ten thirty sharp, Crumb!"

"Sure, ten thirty sharp," repeated Crumb rising. "Oh say, Allen, will you do me a favor? I promised a fellow I'd bring him a bindle of M to-night, and if you'll hand it to him it'll save me the trip. It's right on your way to the car line. You'll find him in the alley back of the Hollywood Drug Store, just west of Cuyhenga on the south side of Hollywood Boulevard."

"Sure, glad to accommodate," said Allen; "but how'll I know him?"

"He'll be standin' there, and you walk up and ask him the time. If he tells you, and then asks if you can change a five, you'll know he's the guy all right. Then you hand him these two ones and a fifty-cent piece, and he hands you a five dollar bill. That's all there is to it. Inside these two ones I'll wrap a bindle of M. You can give me the five Monday morning when I see you"

"Slip me the junk," said Allen.

The girl had risen, and was putting on her coat and hat. "Where are you going—home so early?" asked Crumb.

"Yes," she replied. "I'm tired, and I want to write a letter."

"I thought you lived here," said Allen.

"I'm here nearly all day, but I go home nights," replied the girl.

Slick Allen looked puzzled as he left the bungalow.

"Goin' my way?" he asked of the girl, as they reached the sidewalk.

"No," she replied. "I go in the opposite direction. Good night!"

"Good night!" said Allen, and turned toward Hollywood Boulevard.

Inside the bungalow Crumb was signaling central for a connection.

"Give me the police station on Cuyhenga, near Hollywood," he said. "I haven't time to look up the number. Quick—it's important!"

There was a moment's silence and then:

"Hello! What is this? Listen! If you want to get a hop-head with the goods on him—right in the act of peddling—send a dick to the back of the Hollywood Drug Store, and have him wait there until a guy comes up and asks what time it is. Then have the dick tell him and say, 'Can you change a five?' That's the cue for the guy to slip him a bindle of morphine rolled up in a couple of one-dollar bills. If you don't send a dummy, he'll know what to do next— and you'd better get him there in a hurry. What? No-oh, just a friend just a friend."

Wilson Crumb hung up the receiver. There was a grin on his face as he turned away from the instrument.

"It's too bad, Allen, but I'm afraid you won't be at the bank at half past ten on Monday morning!" he said.

CHAPTER XII

As Gaza de Lure entered the house in which she roomed, her landlady came hastily from the living room.

"Is that you, Miss Burke?" she asked. "Here's a telegram that came for you just a few minutes ago. I do hope it's not bad news!"

"My mother is ill. They have sent for me," said the girl. "I wonder if you would be good enough to call up the S. P. and ask the first train I can get that stops at Ganado, while I run upstairs and pack my bag?"

"You poor little dear!" exclaimed the landlady. "I'm so sorry! I'll call right away, and then I'll come up and help you."

A few minutes later she came up to say that the first train left at nine o'clock in the morning. She offered to help her pack; but the girl said there was nothing that she could not do herself.

"I must go out first for a few minutes," Gaza told her. "Then I will come back and finish packing the few things that it will be necessary to take."

When the landlady had left, the girl stood staring dully at the black traveling bag that she had brought from the closet and placed on her bed; but she did not see the bag or the few pieces of lingerie that she had taken from her dresser drawers. She saw only the sweet face of her mother, and the dear smile that had always shone there to soothe each childish trouble—the smile that had lighted the girl's dark days, even after she had left home.

For a long time she stood there thinking—trying to realize what it would mean to her if the worst should come. It could make no difference, she realized, except that it might perhaps save her mother from a still greater sorrow. It was the girl who was dead, though the mother did not guess it; she had been dead for many months. This hollow, shaking husk was not Shannon Burke—it was not the thing that the mother had loved. It was almost a sacrilege to take it up there into the clean country and flaunt it in the face of so sacred a thing as mother love.

The girl stepped quickly to a writing desk, and, drawing a key from her vanity case, unlocked it. She took from it a case containing a hypodermic syringe and a few small phials; then she crossed the hall to the bathroom. When she came back, she looked rested and less nervous. She returned the things to the desk, locked it, and ran downstairs.

"I will be back in a few minutes," she called to the landlady "I shall have to arrange a few things tonight with a friend."

She went directly to the Vista del Paso bungalow. Crumb was surprised and not a little startled as he heard her key in the door. He had a sudden vision of Allen returning, and he went white; but when he saw who it was he was no less surprised, for the girl had never before returned after leaving for the night.

"My gracious!" he exclaimed. "Look who's here!"

She did not return his smile.

"I found a telegram at home," she said, "that necessitates my going away for a few days. I came over to tell you and, to get a little snow to last me until I come back. Where I am going they don't have it, I imagine."

He looked at her through narrowed, suspicious lids.

"You're going to quit me!" he cried accusingly. "That's why you went out with Allen! You can't get away with it, I'll never let you go. Do you hear me? I'll never let you go!"

"Don't be a fool, Wilson," she replied. "My mother is ill, and I have been sent for."

"Your mother? You never told me you had a mother."

"But I have, though I don't care to talk about her to you. She needs me, and I am going."

He was still suspicious.

"Are you telling the truth? Will you come back?"

"You know I'll come back," she said. "I shall have to," she added with a weary sigh.

"Yes, you'll have to. You can't get along without it. You'll come back all right—I'll see to that!"

"How much snow you got at home?" he demanded.

"You know I keep scarcely any there. I forgot my case to-day—left it in my desk, so I had a little there—a couple of shots, maybe."

"Very well," he said. "I'll give you enough to last a week—then you'll have to come home."

"You say you'll give me enough to last a week?" the girl repeated questioningly. "I'll take what I want—it's as much mine as yours!"

"But you don't get any more than I'm going to give you. I won't have you gone more than a week. I can't live without you—don't you understand? I believe you have a wooden heart, or none at all!"

"Oh," she said, yawning, "you can get some other poor fool to peddle it for you if I don't come back; but I'm coming, never fear. You're as bad as the snow—I hate you both, but I can't live without either of you. I don't feel like quarreling, Wilson. Give me the stuff—enough to last a week, for I'll be home before that."

He went to the bathroom and made a little package up for her.

"Here!" he said, returning to the living room. "That ought to last you a week."

She took it and slipped it into her case.

"Well, good-bye," she said, turning toward the door.

"Aren't you going to kiss me good-bye?" he asked.

"Have I ever kissed you, since I learned that you had a wife?" she asked.

"No," he admitted. "but you might kiss me good-bye now, when you're going away for a whole week."

"Nothing, doing, Wilson!" she said with a negative shake of the head. "I'd as lief kiss a Gila monster!"

He made a wry face.

"You're sure candid," he said.

She shrugged her shoulders in a gesture of indifference and moved toward the door.

On her face was an expression of unspeakable disgust as she passed through the doorway of the bungalow and closed the door behind her. Wilson Crumb simulated a shudder.

"I sure was a damn fool," he mused. "Gaza would have made the greatest emotional actress the screen has ever known, if I'd given her a chance. I guessed her wrong and played her wrong. She's not like any woman I ever saw before. I should have made her a great success and won her gratitude— that's the way I ought to have played her. Oh, well, what's the difference? She'll come back!"

He rose and went to the bathroom, snuffed half a grain of cocaine, and then collected all the narcotics hidden there and every vestige of contributory evidence of their use by the inmates of the bungalow. Dragging a small table into his bedroom closet, he mounted and opened a trap leading into the air space between the ceiling and the roof. Into this he climbed, carrying the drugs with him.

They were wrapped in a long thin package, to which a light, strong cord was attached. With this cord he lowered the package into the space between the sheathing and the inner wall, fastening the end of the cord to a nail driven into one of the studs at arm's length below the wall plate.

"There!" he thought, as he clambered back into the closet. "It'll take some dick to uncover that junk!"

Hidden between plaster and sheathing of the little bungalow was a fortune in narcotics. Only a small fraction of their stock had the two peddlers kept in the bathroom, and Crumb had now removed that, in case Allen should guess that he had been betrayed by his confederate and direct the police to the bungalow, or the police themselves should trace his call and make an investigation on their own account. He realized he had taken a great risk; but his stratagem had saved him from the deadly menace of Allen's vengeance, at least for the present. The fact that there must ultimately be an accounting with the man he put out of his mind. It would be time enough to meet that contingency when it arose.

As a matter of fact, the police came to the bungalow that very evening; but through no clue obtained from Allen, who, while he had suspicions that were tantamount to conviction, chose to await the time when he might wreak his revenge in his own way. The desk sergeant had traced the call to Crumb, and after the arrest had been made a couple of detective sergeants called upon him. They were quiet, pleasant-spoken men, with an ingratiating way that might have deceived the possessor of a less suspicious brain than Crumb's.

"The lieutenant sent us over to thank you for that tip." said the spokesman. "We got him all right, with the junk on him."

Not for nothing was Wilson Crumb a talented actor. None there was who could better have registered polite and uninterested incomprehension.

"I am afraid," he said, "that I don't quite get you. What tip? What are you talking about?"

"You called up the station, Mr. Crumb. We had central trace the call. There is no use—"

Crumb interrupted him with a gesture. He didn't want the officer to go so far that it might embarrass him to retract.

"Ah!" he exclaimed, a light of understanding illuminating his face. "I believe I have it. What was the message? I think I can explain it."

"We think you can, too," agreed the sergeant, "seein' you phoned the message."

"No, but I didn't," said Crumb, "although I guess it may have come over my phone all right. I'll tell you what I know about it. A car drove up a little while after dinner, and a man came to the door. He was a stranger. He asked if I had a phone, and if he could use it. He said he wanted to phone an important and confidential message to his wife. He emphasized the 'confidential,' and there was nothing for me to do but go in the other room until he was through. He wanted to pay for the use of the phone. I didn't hear what he said over the phone, but I guess that explains the matter. I'll be careful next time a stranger wants to use my phone."

"I would," said the sergeant drily. "Would you know him if you saw him again?"

"I sure would," said Crumb.

They rose to go.

"Nice little place you have here," remarked one of them, looking around.

"Yes," said Crumb, "it is very comfortable. Wouldn't you like to look it over?"

"No," replied the officer. "Not now—maybe some other time."

Crumb grinned after he had closed the door behind them.

"I wonder," he mused, "if that was a threat or a prophecy!"

A week later Slick Allen was sentenced to a year in the county jail for having morphine in his possession.

CHAPTER XIII

As Shannon Burke alighted from the Southern Pacific train at Ganado, the following morning, a large middle-aged man in riding clothes approached her.

"Is this Miss Burke?" he asked. "I am Colonel Pennington." She noted that his face was grave, and it frightened her. "Tell me about my mother," she said. "How is she?"

He put an arm about the girl's shoulders.

"Come," he said. "Mrs. Pennington is waiting over at the car." Her question was answered.

"Tell me about it," she said at length in a low voice.

"It was very sudden," said the Colonel. "It was a heart attack. Everything that possibly could be done in so short a time was done. Nothing would have changed the outcome, however. We had Dr. Jones of Los Angeles down—he motored down and arrived here about half an hour before the end. He told us that he could have done nothing."

They were silent for a while as the fast car rolled over the smooth road toward the hills ahead. Presently it slowed down, turned in between orange trees, and stopped before a tiny bungalow a hundred yards from the highway.

"We thought you would want to come here first of all, dear," said Mrs. Pennington. "Afterward we are going to take you home with us."

They accompanied her to the tiny living room, where they introduced her to the housekeeper, and to the nurse, who had remained at Colonel Pennington's request. Then they opened the door of a sunny bedroom, and, closing it after her as she entered left her alone with her dead.

Beyond the thin panels they could hear her sobbing; but when she emerged fifteen minutes later, though her eyes were red, she was not crying.

They led her back to the car, where she sat with wide eyes staring straight ahead. She wanted to scream, to tear her clothing, to do anything but sit there quiet and rigid. The short drive to Ganado seemed to the half mad girl to occupy hours. She saw nothing, not even the quiet, restful ranch house as the car swung up the hill and stopped at the north entrance. In her mind's eye was nothing but the face of her dead mother and the little black case in her traveling bag.

The colonel helped her from the car and a sweet-faced young girl came and put her arms about her and kissed her, as Mrs. Pennington had done at the station. In a dazed sort of way Shannon understood that they were telling her the girl's name—that she was a daughter of the Penningtons. The girl accompanied the visitor to the rooms she was to occupy.

Shannon wished to be alone—she wanted to get at the black case in the traveling bag. Why didn't the girl go away? She wanted to take her by the shoulders and throw her out of the room; yet outwardly she was calm and self-possessed.

Very carefully she turned toward the girl. It required a supreme effort not to tremble, and to keep her voice from rising to a scream.

"Please," she said, "I should like to be alone."

"I understand," said the girl, and left the room, closing the door behind her.

Shannon crept stealthily to the door and turned the key in the lock. Then she wheeled and almost fell upon the traveling bag in her eagerness to get the small black case within it. She was trembling from head to foot, her eyes were wide and staring, and she mumbled to herself as she prepared the white powder and drew the liquid into the syringe.

Momentarily, however, she gathered herself together. For a few seconds she stood looking at the glass and metal instrument in her fingers—beyond it she saw her mother's face.

"I don't want to do it," she sobbed. "I don't want to do it, mother!" Her lower lip quivered, and tears came. "My God, I can't help it!" Almost viciously she plunged the needle beneath her skin. "I didn't want to do it to-day, of all days, with you lying over there all alone—dead!"

She threw herself across the bed and broke into uncontrolled sobbing; but her nerves were relaxed, and the expression of her grief was normal. Finally she sobbed herself to sleep, for she had not slept at all the night before.

It was afternoon when she awoke, and again she felt the craving for a narcotic. This time she did not fight it. She had lost the battle—why renew it? She bathed and dressed and took another shot before leaving her rooms—a guest suite on the second floor. She descended the stairs, which opened directly into the patio, and almost ran against a tall, broad-shouldered young man in flannel shirt and riding breeches, with boots and spurs. He stepped quickly back.

"Miss Burke, I believe?" he inquired. "I am Custer Pennington."

"Oh, it was you who wired me," she said.

"No—that was my father."

"I am afraid I did not thank him for all his kindness. I must have seemed very ungrateful."

She followed him through the living room and the library to the dining room, beyond which a small breakfast room looked out toward the peaceful hills. Young Pennington opened a door leading from the dining room to the butler's pantry, and called to his mother.

"Miss Burke is down," he said.

The girl turned immediately from the breakfast room and entered the butler's pantry.

"Can't I help, Mrs. Pennington? I don't want to go to any trouble for me. You have all been so good already!"

They seemed to take it for granted that Shannon was going to stay with them, instead of going to the little bungalow that had been her mother's—the truest type of hospitality, because, requiring no oral acceptance, it suggested no obligation.

Shannon could not have refused if she had wished to, but she did not wish to. In the quiet ranch house, surrounded by these strong, kindly people, she found a restfulness and a feeling of security that she had not believed she was ever to experience again. She had these thoughts when, under the influence of morphine, her nerves were quieted and her brain clear. After the effects had worn off, she became restless and irritable. She thought of Crumb then, and of the bungalow on the Vista del Paso, with its purple monkeys stenciled over the patio gate. She wanted to be back where she could be free to do as she pleased—free to sink again into the most degrading and abject slavery that human vice has ever devised.

On the first night, after she had gone to her rooms, the Penningtons, gathered in the little family living room, discussed her, as people are wont to discuss a stranger beneath their roof.

"I sized her up over there in the kitchen to-day," said Custer. "She's the real article. I can always tell by the way people treat a servant whether they are real people or only counterfeit. She was as sweet and natural to Hannah as she is to mother."

"I noticed that," said his mother. "It is one of the hall marks of good breeding; but we could scarcely expect anything else of Mrs. Burke's daughter. I know she must be a fine character."

In the room above them Shannon Burke, with trembling hands and staring eyes, was inserting a slender needle beneath the skin above her hip. In the movies one does not disfigure one's arms or legs.

CHAPTER XIV

The day of the funeral had come and gone. It had been a very hard one for Shannon. She had determined that on this day, at least, she would not touch the little hypodermic syringe.

She tried to shut the idea from her mind. She tried to concentrate her thoughts upon the real anguish of her heart. She tried to keep before her a vision of her mother; but her hideous, resistless vice crowded all else from her brain, and the result was that on the way back from the cemetery she collapsed into screaming, incoherent hysteria.

They carried her to her room—Custer Pennington carried her, his father and mother following. When the men had left, Mrs. Pennington and Eva undressed her and comforted her and put her to bed; but she still screamed and sobbed—frightful, racking sobs, without tears. She was trying to tell them to go away. How she hated them! If they would only go away and leave her! But she could not voice the words she sought to scream at them, and so they stayed and ministered to her as best they could. After a while she lost consciousness, and they thought that she was asleep and left her.

Perhaps she did sleep, for later, when she opened her eyes, she lay very quiet, and felt rested and almost normal. She knew, though, that she was not entirely awake—that when full wakefulness came the terror would return unless she quickly had recourse to the little needle.

In that brief moment of restfulness she thought quickly and clearly and very fully of what had just happened. She had never had such an experience before. Perhaps she had never fully realized the frightful hold the drug had upon her. She had known that she could not stop—or, at least, she had said that she knew; but whether she had any conception of the pitiful state to which enforced abstinence would reduce her is to be doubted. Now she knew, and she was terribly frightened.

"I must cut it down," she said to herself. "I must have been hitting it up a little too strong. When I get home, I'll let up gradually until I can manage with three or four shots a day."

When she came down to dinner that night, they were all surprised to see her, for they had thought her still asleep. Particularly were they surprised to see no indications of her recent breakdown. How could they know that she had just taken enough morphine to have killed any one of them? She seemed normal and composed, and she tried to infuse a little gaiety into her conversation, for she realized that her grief was not theirs. She knew that their kind hearts shared something of her sorrow, but it was selfish to impose her own sadness upon them.

She had been thinking very seriously, had Shannon Burke. The attack of hysteria had jarred her loose, temporarily at least, from the selfish rut that her habit and her hateful life with Crumb had worn for her. She recalled every emotion of the ordeal through which she has passed, even to the thoughts of hate that she had held for those two sweet women at the table with her. How could she have hated them? She hated herself for the thought.

She compared herself with them, and a dull flush mounted to her cheek. She was not fit to remain under the same roof with them, and here she was sitting at their table, a respected guest! What if they should learn of the thing she was? The thought terrified her; and yet she talked on, oftentimes gaily, joining with them in the laughter that was part of every meal.

She really saw them, that night, as they were. It was the first time that her grief and her selfish vice, had permitted her to study them. It was her first understanding glimpse of a family life that was as beautiful as her own life was ugly.

As she compared herself with the women, she compared Crumb with these two men. They might have vices—they were strong men, and few strong men are without vices, she knew—but she was sure they were voices of strong men, which, by comparison with those of Wilson Crumb, would become virtues. What a pitiful creature Crumb seemed beside these two, with his insignificant mentality and his petty egotism!

Suddenly it came to her, almost as a shock, that she had to leave this beautiful place and go back to the sordid life that she shared with Crumb. Her spirit revolted but she knew that it must be. She did not belong here—her vice must ever bar her from such men and women as these. The memory of them would haunt her always, making her punishment the more poignant to the day of her death.

That evening she and Colonel Pennington discussed her plans for the future. She had asked him about disposing of the orchard—how she should proceed, and what she might ask for it.

"I should advise you to hold it," he said. "It is going to increase in value tremendously in the next few years. You can easily get some one to work it for you on shares. If you don't want to live on it, Custer and I will be glad to keep an eye on it and see that it is properly cared for; but why don't you stay here? You could really make a very excellent living from it. Besides, Miss Burke, here in the country you can really live. You city people don't know what life is."

"There!" said Eva. "Popsy has started. If he had his way, we'd all have to move to the city to escape the maddening crowd. He'd move the maddening crowd into the country!"

"It may be that Shannon doesn't care for the country," suggested Mrs. Pennington. "There are such foolish people," she added laughing.

"Oh, I would love the country!" exclaimed Shannon.

"Then why don't you stay?" urged the colonel.

"I had never thought of it," she said hesitatingly.

It was indeed a new idea. Of course it was an absolute impossibility, but it was a very pleasant thing to contemplate.

"Possibly Miss Burke has ties in the city that she would not care to break," suggested Custer, noting her hesitation.

Ties in the city! Shackles of iron, rather, she thought bitterly; but, oh, it was such a nice thought! To live here, to see these people daily, perhaps be one of them, to be like them—ah, that would be heaven!

"Yes," she said, "I have ties in the city. I could not remain here, I am afraid, much as I should like to. I—I think I better sell."

"Rubbish!" exclaimed the colonel. "You'll not sell. You are going to stay here with us until you are thoroughly rested and then you won't want to sell."

"I wish that I might," she said; "but—"

"All right," said the colonel. "It's decided—you stay. Now run off to bed, for you're going to ride with us in the morning, and that means that you'll have to be up at half past five."

"But I can't ride," she said. "I don't know how, and I have nothing to wear."

"Eva'll fit you out, and as for not knowing how to ride, you can't learn any younger. Why, I've taught half the children in the foot-hills to ride a horse, and a lot of the grown-ups. What I can't teach you Cus and Eva can. You're going to start in to-morrow, my little girl, and learn how to live. Nobody who has simply survived the counterfeit life of the city knows anything about living. You wait—we'll show you!"

At a quarter before six she was awakened by a knock on her door. It was already light, and she awoke with mingled surprise that she had slept so well and vague forebodings of the next hour or two, for she was unaccustomed to horses and a little afraid of them.

"Who is it?" she asked, as the knock was repeated.

"Eva. I've brought your riding things."

Shannon rose and opened the door. She was going to take the things from the girl, but the latter bounced into the room, fresh and laughing.

"Come on!" she cried. "I'll help you. Just pile your hair up anyhow —it doesn't matter—this hat'll cover it. I think these breeches will fit you—we are just about the same size; but I don't know about the boots—they may be a little large. I didn't bring any spurs —papa won't let any one wear spurs until they ride fairly well. You'll have to win your spurs, you see! It's a beautiful morning just spiffy! Run in and wash up a bit. I'll arrange everything, and you'll be in 'em in a jiffy."

She seized Shannon around the waist and danced off toward the bathroom. "Don't be long," she admonished.

Shannon washed quickly. She was excited at the prospect of the ride. That and the laughing, talking girl in the adjoining room gave her no time to think. Her mind was fully occupied and her nerves were stimulated. For the moment she forgot about morphine, and then it was too late, for Eva had her by the hand and she was being led, almost at a run down the stairs, through the patio, and out over the edge of the hill down toward the stable.

"Fine!" cried the colonel, as he saw her coming. "Really never thought you'd do it! I'll wager this is the earliest you have been up in many a day. 'Barbarous hour'—that's what you're saying. Why, when my cousin was on here from New York, he was really shocked—said it wasn't decent. Come along—we're late this morning. You'll ride Baldy—Custer'll help you up."

She stepped to the mounting block as the young man led the dancing Baldy close beside it.

"Ever ridden much?" he asked.

"Never in my life."

Suddenly it dawned upon her that she had neither fallen off nor come near falling off. She had not even lost a stirrup. As a matter of fact, the motion was not even uncomfortable. It was enjoyable, and she was in about as much danger of being thrown as she would have been from a rocking chair as violently self-agitated. She laughed then, and in the instant all fear left her.

That first morning ride with the Penningtons and their friends was an event in the life of Shannon Burke that assumed the proportions of adventure. The novelty, the thrill, the excitement, filled her every moment. The dancing horse beneath her seemed to impart to her a full measure of its buoyant life. The gay laughter of her companions, the easy fellowship of young and old, the generous sympathy made her one of them, gave her but another glimpse of the possibilities for happiness that requires no artificial stimulus.

That ride ended in a rushing gallop along a quarter mile of straight road leading to the stables, where they dismounted, flushed, breathless, and laughing. As they walked up the winding concrete walk toward the house, Shannon Burke was tired, lame and happy. She had adventured into a new world and found it good.

"Come into my room and wash," said Eva, as they entered the patio. "We're late for breakfast now, and we all like to sit down together."

For just an instant, and for the first time that morning, Shannon thought of the hypodermic needle in its black case upstairs. She hesitated, and then resolutely turned into Eva's room.

CHAPTER XV

During the hour following breakfast that morning, while Shannon was alone in her rooms, the craving returned. The thought of it turned her sick when she felt it coming. She had been occupying herself making her bed and tidying the room, as she had done each morning since her arrival; but when that was done, her thoughts reverted by habit to the desire that had so fatally mastered her.

There crept into her mind a thought that had found its way there more than once during the past two years—the thought of self-destruction. She put it away from her; but in the depth of her soul she knew that never before had it taken so strong a hold upon her. Her mother, her only tie, was gone, and no one would care. She had looked into heaven and found that it was not for her. She had no future except to return to the hideous existence of the Hollywood bungalow and her lonely boarding house, and to the hated Crumb.

It was then that Eva Pennington called her.

She was descending the stairs toward Eva, who stood at the foot, holding open the door that led into the patio. She welcomed the interruption that had broken in upon her morbid thoughts. The sight of the winsome figure smiling up at her dispelled them as the light of the sun sweeps away miasmatic vapors.

They walked down the hill, past the saddle horse barn, and along the graveled road that led to the upper end of the ranch. The summer sun beat hotly upon them, making each old sycamore and oak and walnut a delightful oasis of refreshing shade. In a field at their left two mowers were clicking merrily through lush alfalfa. At their right, beyond the pasture fence, gentle Guernseys lay in the shade of a wide-spreading sycamore, a part of the pastoral allegory of content that was the Rancho del Ganado; and over all were the blue California sky and the glorious sun.

They swung up then through the orange grove, and along the upper road back toward the house. It was noon and lunch time when they arrived. Shannon was hot and tired and dusty and delighted as she opened the door at the foot of the stairs that led to her rooms above.

Then she paused. The old, gripping desire had seized her. She had not once felt it since she had passed through that door more than two hours before. For a moment she hesitated, and then, fearfully, she turned toward Eva.

"May I clean up in your room?" she asked.

There was a strange note of appeal in Shannon's voice that the other girl did not understand.

"Why, certainly," she said; "but is there anything the matter? You are not ill?"

"Just a little tired."

"There! I should never have walked you so far. I'm so sorry!"

"I want to be tired. I want to do it again this afternoon—all afternoon. I don't want to stop until I am ready to drop!" Then, seeing the surprise in Eva's expression, she added: "You see, I shall be here such a short time that I want to crowd every single moment full of pleasant memories."

Shannon thought that she had never eaten so much before as she had that morning at breakfast; but at luncheon she more than duplicated her past performance.

"My!" Shannon exclaimed at last. "I have seen the pigs and I have become one."

"And I see something, dear," said Mrs. Pennington, smiling.

"What?"

"Some color in your cheeks."

"Not really?" she cried, delighted.

"Yes, really."

"And it's mighty becoming," offered the colonel. "Nothing like a brown skin and rosy cheeks for beauty. That's the way God meant girls to be, or He wouldn't have given 'em delicate skins and hung the sun up there to beautify 'em.

"What a dapper little thought!" exclaimed Eva. "Popsy should have been a poet."

"Or an ad writer for a cosmetic manufacturer," suggested Custer. "Oh, by the way, not changing the subject or anything, but did you hear about Slick Allen?"

No, they had not. Shannon pricked up her ears, metaphorically. What did these people know of Slick Allen?

"He's just been sent up in L. A. for having narcotics in his possession. Got a year in the county jail."

"I guess he was a bad one," commented the colonel; "but he never struck me as being a drug addict."

"Nor me; but I guess you can't always tell them," said Custer.

"It must be a terrible habit," said Mrs. Pennington.

"It's about as low as any one can sink," said Custer.

"I hear that there's been a great increase in it since prohibition," remarked the colonel. "Personally, I'd have more respect for a whiskey drunkard than for a drug addict; or perhaps I should better say that I'd feel less disrespect. A police official told me not long ago, at a dinner in town, that if drug-taking continues to increase as it has recently, it will constitute a national menace by comparison with which the whiskey evil will seem paltry."

Shannon Burke was glad when they rose from the table, putting an end to the conversation. She had plumbed the uttermost depths of humiliation. She had felt herself go hot and cold in shame and fear. At first her one thought had been to get away—to find some excuse for leaving the Penningtons at once.

She was hastening to her room to pack. She knew there was an evening train for the city, and while she packed she could be framing some plausible excuse for leaving thus abruptly.

Custer Pennington called to her.

"Miss Burke!" She turned, her hand upon the knob of the door to the upstairs suite.

"I'm going to ride over the back ranch this afternoon. Eva showed you the Berkshires this morning; now I want to show you the Herefords. I told the stableman to saddle Baldy for you. Will half an hour be too soon?"

For a long time they rode in silence, the girl taking in every beauty of meadow, ravine, and hill, that she might store them all away for the days when they would be only memories. The sun beat down upon them fiercely, for it was an early August day, and there was no relieving breeze; but she enjoyed it. It was all so different from any day in her past, and so much happier than anything in the last two years, or anything she could expect in the future.

The riders had entered the hills and were winding up Jackknife Canyon before either spoke.

"If you tire," he said, "or if it gets too hot, we'll turn back. Please don't hesitate to tell me."

"It's heavenly!" she said.

"Possibly a few degrees too hot for heaven," he suggested; "but it's always cool under the live oaks. Any time you want to rest we'll stop for a bit."

"Which are the live oaks?" she asked.

He pointed to one.

"Why are they called live oaks?"

"They're evergreen—I suppose that's the reason. Here's a big old fellow—shall we stop?"

"And get off?"

"If you wish."

"Do you think I could get on again?"

Pennington laughed.

After a while they started on again, and the girl surprised the man by mounting easily from the ground. She was very much pleased with her achievement, laughing happily at his word of approval.

They rode on until they found the Herefords. They counted them as they searched through the large pasture that ran back into the hills; and when the full number had been accounted for, they turned toward home. As he had told her about the trees, Custer told her also about the beautiful white-faced cattle, of their origin in the English county whose name they bear, and of their unequaled value as beef animals. He pointed out various prize winners as they passed them.

"There you are, smiling again," she said accusingly, as they followed the trail homeward. "What have I done now?"

"You haven't done anything but be very patient all afternoon. I was smiling at the idea of how thrilling the afternoon must have been for a city girl, accustomed, I suppose, to a constant round of pleasure and excitement!"

"I have never known a happier afternoon," she said.

"I wonder if you really mean that?"

"Honestly!"

"I am glad," he said: "for sometimes I get terribly tired of it here, and I think it always does me good to have an outsider enthuse a little. It brings me a realization of the things we have here that city people can't have, and makes me a little more contented."

"You couldn't be discontented! Why, there are just thousands and thousands of people in the city who would give everything to change places with you! We don't all live in the city because we want to. You are fortunate that you don't have to."

"Do you think so?"

"I know it."

"But it seems such a narrow life here! I ought to be doing a man's work among men, where it will count. "

"You are doing a man's work here and living a man's life, and what you do here does count. Suppose you were making stoves, or selling automobiles or bonds, in the city. Would any such work count for more than all this—the wonderful swine and cattle and horses that you are raising? Your father has built a great business, and you are helping him to make it greater. Could you do anything in the city of which you could be half so proud? No, but in the city you might find a thousand things to do of which you might be terribly ashamed. If I were a man, I'd like your chance!"

"You're not consistent. You have the same chance, but you tell us that you are going back to the city. You have your grove here, and a home and good living, and yet you want to return to the city you inveigh against."

"I do not want to," she declared.

"I hope you don't, then," Custer said simply.

They reached the house in time for a swim before dinner; but after dinner, when they started for the ballroom to dance, Shannon threw up her hands in surrender.

"I give up!" she cried laughingly. "I tried to be game to the finish, and I want ever so much to come and dance; but I don't believe I could even walk as far as the ballroom, much less dance after I got there. Why, I doubt whether I'll be able to get upstairs without crawling!"

"You poor child!" exclaimed Mrs. Pennington. "We've nearly killed you, I know. We are all so used to the long rides and walking and swimming and dancing that we don't realize how they tire unaccustomed muscles. You go right to bed, my dear, and don't think of getting up for breakfast."

"Oh, but I want to get up and ride, if I may, and if Eva will wake me."

"She's got the real stuff in her;" commented the colonel, after Shannon had bid them good night and gone to her rooms.

"I'll say she has," agreed Custer. "She's a peach of girl!"

"She's simply divine," added Eva.

In her room, Shannon could barely get into bed before she was asleep.

CHAPTER XVI

It was four o'clock the following morning before she awoke. The craving awoke with her. It seized her mercilessly; yet even as she gave in to it, she had the satisfaction of knowing that she had gone without the little white powders longer this time than since she had first started to use them. She took but a third of her normal dose.

That day she went with Custer and Eva and Guy to the country club, returning only in time for a swim before dinner; and again she fought off the craving while she was dressing for dinner. After dinner they danced, and once more she was so physically tired when she reached her rooms that she could think of nothing but sleep. The day of golf had kept her fully occupied in the hot sun, and in such good company her mind had been pleasantly occupied, too, so that she had not been troubled by her old enemy.

Again it was early morning before she was forced to fight the implacable foe. She fought valiantly this time, but she lost.

And so it went, day after day, as she dragged out her dwindling supply and prolonged the happy hours of her all too brief respite from the degradation of the life to which she knew she must soon return. Each day it was harder to think of going back—of leaving these people, whom she had come to love as she loved their lives and surroundings, and taking her place again in the stifling and degraded atmosphere of the Vista del Paso bungalow. They were so good to her, and had so wholly taken her into their family life, that she felt as one of them. They shared everything with her. There was not a day that she did not ride with Custer out among the brown hills. She knew that she was going to miss these rides—that she was going to miss the man, too. He had treated her as a man would like other men to treat his sister, with a respect and deference that she had never met with in the City of Angels.

And now the time had come when she must definitely set a date for her departure. She had determined to retain the orchard, not alone because she had seen that it would prove profitable, but because it would always constitute a link between her and the people whom she had come to love. No matter what the future held, she could always feel that a part of her remained here, where she would that all of her might be; but she knew that she must go, and she determined to tell them on the following day that she would return to the city within the week.

She passed that night without recourse to the white powders, for she must be frugal of them if they were to last through the week. The next morning she rode with the Penningtons and the Evanses as usual. She would tell them at breakfast.

When she came to the table she found a pair of silver spurs beside her plate, and when she looked about in astonishment they were all smiling.

"For me?" she cried.

After that she simply couldn't tell them then that she was going away. She would wait until tomorrow; but she laid her plans without reference to the hand of fate.

That afternoon, immediately after luncheon, they were all seated in the patio, lazily discussing the chief topic of thought—the heat. It was one of those sultry days that are really unusual in southern California. The heat was absolutely oppressive, and even beneath the canvas canopy that shaded the patio there was little relief.

"I don't know why we sit here," said Custer. "It's cooler in the house. This is the hottest place on the ranch a day like this!"

"Wouldn't it be nice under one of those oaks up the canyon?" suggested Shannon.

He looked at her and smiled.

"Phew! It's too hot even to think of getting there."

"That from a Pennington!" she cried in mock astonishment and reproach.

"Do you mean to say that you'd ride up there through this heat?" he demanded.

"Of course I would. I haven't christened my new spurs yet."

"I'm game, then, if you are," Custer announced.

She jumped to her feet.

It was very hot. The dust rose from the shuffling feet of their horses. Even the Apache shuffled today. His head was low, and he did not dance. The dust settled on sweating neck and flank, and filled the eyes of the riders.

"Lovely day for a ride," commented Custer.

"But think how nice it will be under the oak," she reminded him.

"I'm trying to."

Suddenly he raised his head as his wandering eyes sighted a slender column of smoke rising from behind the ridge beyond Jackknife Canyon. He reined in the Apache.

"Fire!" he said to the girl. "Wait here. I'll notify the boys, and then we'll ride on ahead and have a look at it. It may not amount to anything."

Presently the "boys"—a wagon full of them—came with four horses, two walking plows, shovels, a barrel of water, and burlap sacks. They were of all ages, from eighteen to seventy. Some of them had been twenty years on the ranch, and had fought many a fire. They did not have to be told what to bring or what to do with what they brought.

The wagon had to be left in Jackknife Canyon. The horses dragged the plows to the ridge, and the men carried the shovels and wet burlaps and buckets of water from the barrel. Custer dismounted and turned the Apache over to an old man to hold.

"Plow down the east side of the ravine. Try to get all the way around the south side of the fire and then back again," he directed the two men with one of the teams. "I'll take the other, with Jake, and we'll try to cut her off across the top here!"

"You can't do it, Cus," said one of the older men. "It's too steep."

"We've got to try it," said Pennington. "Otherwise we'd have to go back so far that it would get away from us on the east side before we made the circle. Jake, you choke the plow handles—I'll drive!"

Jake was a short, stocky, red-headed boy of twenty, with shoulders like a bull. He grinned good-naturedly.

"I'll choke the tar out of 'em!" he said.

"The rest of you shovel and beat like hell!" ordered Custer.

They were more than halfway back when it happened. The off horse must have stepped upon a loose stone, so suddenly did he lurch to to the left, striking the shoulder of his mate just as the latter had planted his left forefoot. The ton of weight hurled against the shoulder of the near horse threw him downward against the furrow. He tried to catch himself on his right foot, crossed his forelegs, stumbled over the ridge of newly turned earth, and rolled down the hill, dragging his mate and the plow after him toward the burning brush below.

Jake at the plow handles and Custer on the lines tried to check the horses' fall, but both were jerked from their hands, and the two Percherons rolled over and over into the burning brush. A groan of dismay went up from the men. It was with difficulty that Shannon stifled a scream; and then her heart stood still as she saw Custer Pennington leap deliberately down the hillside, drawing the long, heavy trail-cutting knife that he always wore on the belt with his gun.

The horses were struggling and floundering to gain their feet. One of them was screaming with pain. The girl wanted to cover her eyes with her palms to shut out the heart-rending sight, but she could not take them off the figure of the man.

As Shannon watched, a great light awoke within her, suddenly revealing the unsuspected existence of a wondrous thing that had come into her life— a thing which a moment later dragged her from her saddle and sent her stumbling down the hill into the burning ravine, to the side of Custer Pennington.

He had cut one horse free, seized its headstall, dragged it to its feet, and then started it scrambling up the hill. As he was returning to the other, the animal struggled up, crazed with terror and pain, and bolted after its mate. Pennington was directly in its path on the steep hillside. He tried to leap aside, but the horse struck him with its shoulder, hurling him to the ground, and before he could stop his fall he was at the edge of the burning brush, stunned and helpless.

Every man of them who saw the accident leaped down the hillside to save him from the flames; but quick as they were, Shannon Burke was first to his side, vainly endeavoring to drag him to safety. An instant later strong hands seized both Custer and Shannon and helped them up the steep acclivity, for Pennington had already regained consciousness, and it was not necessary to carry him.

Custer was badly burned, but his first thought was for the girl, and his next when he found she was uninjured, for the horses.

Then he turned to Shannon.

"Why did you go down into that?" he asked. "You shouldn't have done it—with all the men here."

"I couldn't help it," she said. "I thought you were going to be killed."

Custer looked at her searchingly for a moment.

"It was very brave thing to do," he said, "and a very foolish thing. You might have been badly burned."

"Never mind that," she said. "You have been badly burned, and you must go to the house at once. Do you think you can ride?" He laughed.

"I'm all right," he said. "I've got to stay here and fight this fire."

"You are not going to do anything of the kind." She turned and called to the man who held Pennington's horse. "Please bring the Apache over here," she said. "These men can fight the fire without you," she told Custer. "You are going right back with me. You're never seen any one badly burned, or you'd know how necessary it is to take care of burns at once."

He was not accustomed to being ordered about, and it amused him. Grace would never have thought of questioning his judgment in this or any other matter; but this girl's attitude implied that she considered his judgment faulty and his decisions of no consequence. She evidently had the courage of her convictions, for she caught up her own horse and rode over to the men, who had resumed their work, to tell them that Custer was too badly burned to remain with them.

"I told him that he must go back to the house and have his burns dressed; but he doesn't want to. Maybe he would pay more attention to you, if you told him."

"Sure, we'll tell him," cried one of them. "Here comes Colonel Pennington now. He'll make him go, if it's necessary."

Colonel Pennington reined in a dripping horse beside his son, and Shannon rode over to them. Custer was telling him about the accident to the team.

"Burned, was he?" exclaimed the colonel. "Why damn it, man, you're burned!"

"It's nothing," replied the younger man.

"It is something, colonel," cried Shannon. "Please make him go back to the house. He won't pay any attention to me, and he ought to be cared for right away. He should have a doctor just as quickly as we can get one."

"Can you ride?" snapped the colonel at Custer.

"Of course I can ride!"

"Then get out of here and take care of yourself. Will you go with him, Shannon? Have them call Dr. Baldwin."

As the horses moved slowly along the dusty trail, Shannon, riding a pace behind the man, watched his profile for signs of pain, that she knew he must be suffering. Once, when he winced, she almost gave a little cry, as if it had been she who was tortured. They were riding very close, and she laid her hand gently upon his right arm, in sympathy.

"I am so sorry!" she said. "I know it must pain you terribly."

He turned to her with a smile on his face, now white and drawn.

"It does hurt a little now," he said.

By the time they reached the house she could see that the man was suffering excruciating pain. The stableman had gone to help the fire fighters, as had every able-bodied man on the ranch, so that she had to help Custer from the Apache. After tying the two horses at the stable, she put an arm about him and assisted him up the long flight of steps to the house. There Mrs. Pennington and Hannah came at her call and took him to his room, while she ran to the office to telephone for the doctor.

When she returned, they had Custer undressed and in bed, and were giving such first aid as they could. She stood in the doorway for a moment, watching him, as he fought to hide the agony he was enduring. He rolled his head slowly from side to side, as his mother and Hannah worked over him; but he stifled even a faint moan, though Shannon knew that his tortured body must be goading him to screams. He opened his eyes and saw her, and tried to smile.

Mrs. Pennington turned then and discovered her.

"Please let me do something, Mrs. Pennington, if there is anything I can do."

"I guess we can't do much until the doctor comes. If we only had something to quiet the pain until then!"

If they only had something to quiet the pain. The horror of it! She had something that would quiet the pain; but at what a frightful cost to herself must she divulge it! They would know then, the sordid story of her vice. There could be no other explanation of her having such an outfit in her possession. How they would loathe her! To see disgust in the eyes of these friends, whose good opinion was her one cherished longing, seemed a punishment too great to bear.

And then there was the realization of that new force that had entered her life with the knowledge that she loved Custer Pennington. It was a hopeless love, she knew; but she might at least have had the happiness of knowing that he respected her. Was she to be spared nothing? Was her sin to deprive her of even the respect of the man she loved?

She saw him lying there, and saw the muscles of his jaws tensing as he battled to conceal his pain; and then she turned and ran up the stairway to her rooms. She did not hesitate again, but went directly to her bag, unlocked it, and took out the little black case. Carefully she dissolved a little of the white powder—a fraction of what she could have taken without danger of serious results, but enough to allay his suffering until the doctor came. She knew that this was the end— that she might not remain under that roof another night.

She drew the liquid through the needle into the glass barrel of the syringe, wrapped it in her handkerchief, and descended the stairs. She felt as if she moved in a dream. She felt that she was not Shannon Burke at all, but another whom Shannon Burke watched with pitying eyes; for it did not seem possible that she could enter that room and before his eyes and Mrs. Pennington's and Hannah's reveal the thing that she carried in her handkerchief.

Ah, the pity of it! To realize her first love, and in the same hour to slay the respect of its object with her own hand! Yet she entered the room with a brave step, fearlessly. Had he not risked his life for the two dumb brutes he loved? Could she be less courageous? Perhaps though, she was braver, for she was knowingly surrendering what was dearer to her than life.

Mrs. Pennington turned toward her as she entered.

"He has fainted," she said. "My poor boy!"

Tears stood in his mother's eyes.

"He is not suffering, then?" asked Shannon, trembling.

"Not now. For his sake, I hope he won't recover consciousness until after the doctor comes."

Shannon Burke staggered and would have fallen had she not grasped the frame of the door.

It was not long before the doctor came, and then she went back up the stairs to her rooms, still trembling. She took the filled hypodermic syringe from her handkerchief and looked at it. Then she carried it into the bathroom.

"You can never tempt me again," she said aloud, as she emptied its contents into the lavatory. "Oh, dear God, I love him!"

CHAPTER XVII

That night Shannon insisted upon taking her turn at Custer's bedside, and she was so determined that they could not refuse her. He was still suffering, but not so acutely. The doctor had left morphine, with explicit directions for its administration should it be required. The burns, while numerous, and reaching from his left ankle to his cheek, were superficial, and, though painful, not necessarily dangerous.

He slept but little, and when he was awake he wanted to talk. He told her about Grace. It was his first confidence—a sweetly sad one— for he was a reticent man concerning those things that were nearest his heart and consequently the most sacred to him. He had not heard from Grace for some time, and her mother had had but one letter—a letter that had not sounded like Grace at all. They were anxious about her.

"I wish she would come home!" he said wistfully. "You would like her, Shannon. We could have such bully times together! I think I would be content here if Grace were back; but without her it seems very different, and very lonely. You know we have always been together, all of us, since we were children— Grace, Eva, Guy, and I; and now that you are here it would be better, for you are just like us. You seem like us, at least—as if you had always lived here, too."

"It's nice to have you say that; but I haven't always been here, and, really, you know I don't belong. "

"But you do belong!"

"And I'm going away again pretty soon. I must go back to the city."

"Please don't go back," he begged. "You don't really have to, do you?"

"I had intended telling you all this morning; but after the spurs, I couldn't."

"Do you really have to go?" Custer insisted.

"I don't have to, but I think I ought to. Do you want me to stay—honestly?"

"Honest Injun!" he said, smiling.

"Maybe I will."

He could have voiced no higher praise.

He asked about the fire, and especially about the horses. He was delighted when she told him that a man had just come down to say that the fire was practically out, and the colonel was coming in shortly; and that the veterinary had been there and found the team not seriously injured.

"I think that fire was incendiary," he said; "but now that Slick Allen is in jail, I don't know who would set it."

"Who is Slick Allen," she asked, "and why should he want to set fire to Ganado?"

He told her, and she was silent for a while, thinking about Allen and the last time she had seen him. She wondered what he would do when he got out of jail. She would hate to be in Wilson Crumb's boots then, for she guessed that Allen was a hard character.

While she was thinking of Allen, Custer mentioned Guy Evans. Instantly there came to her mind, for the first time since that last evening at the Vista del Paso bungalow, Crumb's conversation with Allen and the latter's account of the disposition of the stolen whiskey. His very words returned to her.

"Got a young high-blood at the edge of the valley handling it—a fellow by the name of Evans."

She had not connected Allen or that conversation or the Evans he had mentioned with these people; but now she knew that it was Guy Evans who was disposing of the stolen liquor. She wondered if Allen would return to this part of the country after he was released from jail. If he did, and saw her, he would be sure to recognize her, for he must have had her features impressed upon his memory by the fact that she so resembled some one he had known.

If he recognized her, would he expose her? She did not doubt but that he would. The chances were that he would attempt to blackmail her; but, worst of all, he might tell Crumb where she was. That was the thing she dreaded most—seeing Wilson Crumb again, or having him discover her whereabouts; for she knew that he would leave no stone unturned and hesitate to stoop to no dishonorable act, to get her back again. She shuddered when she thought of him—a man whose love, even, was a dishonorable and dishonoring thing.

Then she turned her eyes to the face of the man lying there on the bed beside which she sat. He would never love her; but her love for him had already ennobled her.

Custer moved restlessly. Again he was giving evidence of suffering. She laid a cool palm upon his forehead, and stroked it. He opened his eyes and smiled up at her.

"It's bully of you to sit with me," he said; "but you ought to be in bed. You've had a pretty hard day, and you're not as used to it as we are."

"I am not tired," she said, "and I should like to stay—if you would like to have me."

He took her hand from his forehead and kissed it.

"Of course I like to have you here, Shannon—you're just like a sister. It's funny, isn't it, that we should all feel that way about you, when we've only known you a few weeks? It must have been because of the way you fitted in. You belonged right from the start—you were just like us."

She turned her head away suddenly, casting her eyes upon the floor and biting her lip to keep back the tears.

"What's the matter?" he asked.

"I am not like you, Custer; but I have tried to be."

"Why aren't you like us?" he demanded.

"I—-why, I—couldn't ride a horse," she explained lamely.

"Don't make me laugh, please; my face is burned," he pleaded in mock irony. "Do you think that's all we know, or think of, or possess—our horsemanship? We have hearts, and minds, such as they are—and souls, I hope. It was of these things that I was thinking. I was thinking too, that we Penningtons demand a higher standard in women than is customary nowadays. We are a little old-fashioned, I guess. We want the blood of our horses and the minds of our women pure. Here is a case in point—I can tell you, because you don't know the girl and never will. She was the daughter of a friend of Cousin William—our New York cousin. She was spending the winter in

Pasadena, and we had her out here on Cousin William's account. She was a pippin of a looker, and I suppose she was all right morally; but she didn't have a clean mind. I discovered it about the first time I talked with her alone; and Eva asked me a question about something that she couldn't have known about at all except through this girl. I didn't know what to do. She was a girl and so I couldn't talk about her to any one, not even my father or mother; but I didn't want her around Eva. I wondered if I was just a narrow prig, and if, after all, there was nothing that any one need take exception to in the girl. I got to analyzing the thing, and I came to the conclusion that I would be ashamed of mother and Eva if they talked or thought along such lines. Consequently, it wasn't right to expose Eva to that influence. That was what I decided, and I don't just think I was right—I know I was."

"And what did you do?" Shannon asked in a very small voice.

"I did what under any other circumstances would have been unpardonable. I went to the girl and asked her to make some excuse that would terminate her visit. It was a very hard thing to do; but I would do more than that— I would sacrifice my most cherished friendship—for Eva."

"And the girl—did you tell her why you asked her to go?"

"I didn't want to, but she insisted, and I told her."

"Did she understand?"

"She did not."

They were silent for some time.

"Do you think I did wrong?" he asked.

"No. There is mental virtue as well as physical. It is as much your duty to protect your sister's mind as to protect her body."

"I knew you'd think as I do about it; but let me tell you it was an awful jolt to the cherished Pennington hospitality. I hope I never have to do it again!"

"I hope you never do."

He commenced to show increasing signs of suffering, presently, and then he asked for morphine.

"I don't want to take it unless I have to," he explained.

"No," she said, "do not take it unless you have to."

She prepared and administered it, but she felt no desire for it herself. Then Eva came to relieve her, and she bade them good night and went up to bed. She awoke about four o'clock in the morning, and immediately thought of the little black case; but she only smiled, turned over, and went back to sleep again.

CHAPTER XVIII

It was several weeks before Custer could ride again, and in the meantime Shannon had gone down to her own place to live. She came up every day on Baldy, who had been loaned to her until Custer should be able to select a horse for her. She insisted that she would own nothing but a Morgan, and that she wanted one of the Apache's brothers.

"You'll have to wait, then, until I can break one for you," Custer told her. "There are a couple of four-year-olds that are saddle-broke and bridle-wise in a way; but I wouldn't want you to ride either of them until they've had the finishing touches. I want to ride them enough to learn their faults, if they have any. In the meantime you just keep Baldy down there and use him. How's ranching? You look as if it agreed with you. Nobody'd know you for the same girl. You look like an Indian, and how your cheeks have filled out!"

The girl smiled happily. Her cheeks were flushed, her eyes dancing. She was a picture of life and health and happiness; and Custer's eyes were sparkling, too.

"Gee!" he exclaimed. "You're a regular Pennington!"

"I wish I were!" the girl thought to herself. "You honor me," was what she said aloud.

Custer laughed.

"That sounded rotten, didn't it? But you know what I meant—it's nice to have people whom we like like the same things we do. It doesn't necessarily mean that we think our likes are the best in the world. I didn't mean to be egotistical."

Eva had just entered the patio. She walked over and perched on his knee and kissed him.

"Do you know, I think I'll go on the stage or the screen—wouldn't it be splishous, though?—'Miss Eva Pennington is starring in the new and popular success based on the story by Guy Thackeray Evans, the eminent author!' "

"Oh, Eva!" cried Shannon, genuine concern in her tone. "Surely you wouldn't think of the screen, would you? You're not serious?"

"Oh, yes," said Custer. "She's serious—serious is her middle name. To-morrow she will want to be a painter, and day after to-morrow the world's most celebrated harpist. Eva is nothing if not serious, while her tenacity of purpose is absolutely inspiring. Why, once, for one whole day, she wanted to do the same thing."

Eva was laughing with her brother and Shannon.

"If she were just like every one else, you wouldn't love your little sister any more," she said, running her fingers through his hair. "Honestly, ever since I met Wilson Crumb, I have thought I should like to be a movie star."

"Wilson Crumb!" exclaimed Shannon. "What do you know of Wilson Crumb?"

"Oh, I've met him," said Eva airily. "Don't you envy me?"

"What do you know about him, Shannon?" asked Custer. "Your tone indicated that you may have heard something about him that wasn't complimentary."

"No—I don't know him. It's only what I've heard. I don't think you'd like him." Shannon almost shuddered at the thought of this dear child even so much as knowing Wilson Crumb. "Oh, Eva!" she cried impulsively. "You mustn't even think of going into pictures. I lived in Los Angeles long enough to learn that the life is oftentimes a hard one, filled with disappointment, disillusionment, and regrets— principally regrets."

"And Grace is there now," said Custer in a low voice, a worried look in his eyes.

"Can't you persuade her to return?"

He shook his head.

"It wouldn't be fair," he said. "She is trying to succeed, and we ought to encourage her. It is probably hard enough for her at best, without all of us suggesting antagonism to her ambition by constantly urging her to abandon it, so we try to keep our letters cheerful."

"Have you been to see her since she left? No, I know you haven't. If I were you, I'd run down to L.A. It might mean a lot to her, Custer; it might mean more than you can guess."

The girl spoke from a full measure of bitter experience. She realized what it might have meant to her had there been some man like this to come to her when she had needed the strong arm of a clean love to drag her from the verge of the mire. She would have gone away with such a man—gone back home, and thanked God for the opportunity. If Grace loved Custer, and was encountering the malign forces that had arisen from their own corruption to claw at Shannon's skirts, she would come back with him.

"You really think I ought to go?" Custer asked. "You know she has insisted that none of us should come. She said she wanted to do it all on her own, without any help. Grace is not only very ambitious, but very proud. I'm afraid she might not like it."

"I wouldn't care what she liked," said Shannon. "Either you or Guy should run down there and see her. You are the two men most vitally interested in her. No girl should be left alone long in Hollywood without some one to whom she can look for the right sort of guidance and— and— protection."

"I believe I'll do it," said Custer. "I can't get away right now; but I'll run down there before I go on to Chicago with the show herds for the International."

As a small boy, it had been Custer's duty, as well as his pleasure, to "ride fence." During his enforced idleness, while recovering from his burns, the duty had devolved upon Jake. On the first day that Custer took up the work again, Jake had called his attention to a matter that had long been a subject of discussion and conjecture on the part of the employees.

"There's something funny goin' on back in them hills," said Jake. "I've seen fresh signs every week of horses and burros comin' and goin'. Sometimes they trail through El Camino Largo and again through Corto. An' they've even been down through the old goat corral once, plumb through the ranch, an' out the west gate. But what I can't tell for sure is whether they come in an' go out, or go out an' come in. Whoever does it is foxy. Their two trails never cross, an' they must be made within a few hours of each other, for I'm not Injun enough to tell which is freshest—the one comin' to Ganado or the one goin' out. An' then they muss it up by draggin' brush, so it's hard to tell how many they be of 'em. It's got me."

"They head for Jackknife, don't they?" asked Custer.

"Sometimes, an' sometimes they go straight up Sycamore, an' again they head in or out of half a dozen different little barrancos comin' down from the east; but sooner or later I lose 'em—can't never follow 'em no place in particular. Looks like as if they split up."

"Maybe it's only greasers from the valley coming up after firewood at night."

"Mebbe," said Jake; "but that don't sound reasonable."

"I know it doesn't; but I can't figure out what else it can be. I found a trail up above Jackknife last spring, and maybe that had something to do with it. I've sure got to follow that up. The trouble has been that it doesn't lead where the stock ever goes, and I haven't had time to look into it. Do you think they come up here regularly?"

"We got it doped out that it's always Friday nights. I see the tracks Saturday mornings, and some of the boys say they've heard 'em along around midnight a couple of times."

"What gates do they go out by?"

"They use all four of 'em at different times."

"H-m! Padlock all the gates tomorrow. This is Thursday. Then we'll see what happens."

They did see, for on the following Saturday, when Custer rode fence, he found it cut close by one of the padlocked gates—the gate that opened into the mouth of Horse Camp Canyon. Shannon was with him, and she was much excited at this evidence of mystery so close to home.

"What in the world do you suppose they can be doing?" she asked.

"I don't know; but it's something they shouldn't be doing, or they wouldn't go to so much pains to cover their tracks. They evidently passed in and out at this point, but they've brushed out their tracks on both sides, so that you can't tell which way they went last. Look here! On both sides of the fence the trail splits.

It's hard to say which was made first, and where they passed through the fence. One track must have been on top of the other, but they've brushed it out."

He had dismounted, and was on his knees, examining the spoor beyond the fence.

"I believe," he said presently, "that the fresher trail is the one going toward the hills, although the other one is heavier. Here's a rabbit track that lies on top of the track of a horse's hoof pointed toward the valley, and over here a few yards the same rabbit track is obliterated by the track of horses and burros coming up from the valley. The rabbit must have come across here after they went down, stepping on top of their tracks, and when they came up again they crossed on top of his. That's pretty plain, isn't it?"

"Yes; but the tracks going down are much plainer than those going up. Wouldn't that indicate that they were fresher?"

"That's what I thought until I saw this evidence introduced by Brer Rabbit —and it's conclusive, too. Let's look along here a little farther. I have an idea that I have an idea." He bent close above first one trail and then another, following them down toward the valley.

"I think I've got a line on it," he said presently. "Two men rode along here on horses. One horse was shod, the other was not. One rider went ahead, the other brought up the rear, and between them were several burros. Going down, the burros carried heavy loads; coming back, they carried nothing."

"How do you know all that?" she asked rather incredulously.

"I don't know it, but it seems the most logical deduction from these tracks. It is easy to tell the horse tracks from those of the burros, and to tell that there were at least two horses, because it is plain that a shod horse and an unshod horse passed along here. That one horse—the one with shoes—went first is evident from the fact that you always see the imprints of burro hoofs, or the hoofs of an unshod horse, or both superimposed on his. That the other horse brought up the rear is equally plain from the fact that no other tracks lie on top of his. Now, if you will look close, and compare several of these horse tracks, you will notice that there is little or no difference in the appearance of those leading into the valley and those leading out; but you can see that the burro tracks leading down are more deeply imprinted than those leading up. To me that means that those burros carried heavy loads down and came back light. How does it sound?"

"It's wonderful!" she exclaimed. "It is all that I can do to see that anything has been along here."

"There is nothing very remarkable about it. Just look at the Apache's hoofprints, for instance. See how the hind differ from the fore." Custer pointed to them as he spoke, calling attention to the fact that the Apache's hind shoes were squared off at the toe.

"And now compare them with Baldy's," he said. "See how different the two hoofprints are. Once you know them, you could never confuse one with the other. But the part of the story that would interest me most I can't read—who they are, what they were packing out of the hills on these burros, where they come from, and where they went. Let's follow down and see where they went in the valley. The trail must pass right by the Evanses' hay barn."

The Evanses' hay barn! A great light illuminated Shannon's memory. Allen had said, that last night at the bungalow, that the contraband whiskey was hauled away on a truck, that it was concealed beneath hay, and that a young man named Evans handled it.

What was she to do? She dared not reveal this knowledge to Custer, because she could not explain how she came into possession of it. Nor, for the same reason, could she warn Guy Evans, had she thought that necessary— which she was sure it was not, since Custer would not expose him. She concluded that all she could do was to let events take their own course.

She followed Custer as he traced the partially obliterated tracks through a field of barley stubble. A hundred yards west of the hay barn the trail entered a macadam road at right angles, and there it disappeared. There was no telling whether the little caravan had turned east or west, for it left no spoor upon the hard surface of the paved road.

"Well, Watson!" said Custer, turning to her with a grin. "What do you make of this?"

"Nothing."

"Nothing? Watson, I am surprised. Neither do I." He turned his horse back toward the cut fence. "There's no use looking any farther in this direction. I don't know that it's even worth while following the trail back into the hills, for the chances are that they have it well covered. What I'll do is to lay for them next Friday night. Maybe they're not up to any mischief, but it looks suspicious; and if they are, I'd rather catch them here with the goods than follow them up into the hills, where about all I'd accomplish would probably be to warn them that they were being watched. I'm sorry now I had those gates locked, for it will have put them on their guard. We'll just fix up this fence, and then we'll ride about and take all the locks off."

"You'll not wait for them alone?" she asked, for she knew what he did not —that they were probably unscrupulous rascals who would not hesitate to commit any crime if they thought themselves in danger of discovery.

"Why not?" he asked. "I only want to ask them what they are doing on Ganado, and why they cut our fence."

"Please don't!" she begged. "You don't know who they are or what they have been doing. They might be very desperate men, for all we know."

"All right," he agreed. "I'll take Jake with me."

"Why don't you get Guy to go along, too?" she suggested, for she knew that he would be safer if Guy knew of his intention, since then there would be little likelihood of his meeting the men.

"No," he replied. "Guy would have to have a big camp fire, an easy chair, and a package of cigarettes if he was going to sit up that late out in the hills. Jake's the best for that sort of work."

"Guy isn't a bit like you, is he?" she asked. "He's lived right here and led the same sort of life, and yet he doesn't seem to be a part of it, as you are."

"Guy's a dreamer, and he likes to be comfortable all the time," laughed Custer.

"But perhaps Guy would like the adventure of it," she insisted. "It might give him material for a story. I'm going to ask him."

"You won't mention it to him, please?" Custer insisted.

"Not if you don't wish it," she said.

They were silent for a time, each absorbed in his or her own thoughts. The girl was seeking to formulate some plan that would prevent a meeting between Custer and Allen's confederates, who she was sure were the owners of the mysterious pack train; while the man indulged in futile conjectures as to their identity and the purpose of their nocturnal expeditions.

"That trail above Jackknife Canyon is the key to the whole business," he declared presently. "I'll just lay low until after next Friday night, so as not to arouse their suspicions, and then, no matter what I find out, I'll ride that trail to its finish, if it takes me clear to the ocean!"

CHAPTER XIX

Shannon Burke did not ride to her home after she left Custer. She turned toward the west at the road above the Evans place, continued on to the mouth of Horse Camp Canyon, and entered the hills. For two miles she followed the canyon trail to El Camino Largo, and there, turning to the left, she followed this other trail east to Sycamore Canyon. Whatever her mission, it was evident that she did not wish it known to others. Had she not wished to conceal it, she might have ridden directly up Sycamore Canyon from Ganado with a saving of several miles.

Presently she found what she sought—a trail running north and south across the basin. She turned Baldy into it, and headed him south toward the mountains. She was nervous and inwardly terrified, and a dozen times she would have turned back had she not been urged on by a power infinitely more potent than self-interest.

She had found what she sought, but the fear that rode her all but sent her panic-stricken in retreat. It was only the fact that she could not turn Baldy upon that narrow trail that gave her sufficient pause to gain mastery over the chaos of her nerves and drive them again into the fold of reason. It required a supreme effort of will to urge her horse onward again, down into that mysterious ravine, where she knew there might lurk for her a thing more terrible than death. That she did it bespoke the greatness of the love that inspired her courage.

After what seemed a long time she rode out among splendid old oaks, in view of a soiled tent and a picket line where three horses and a half dozen burros were tethered. Nowhere was there sign of the actual presence of men, yet she had an uncanny feeling that they were there, and that from some place of concealment they were watching her. She sat quietly upon her horse for a moment, waiting. Then, no one appearing, she called aloud.

"Hello, there! I want to speak with you."

Her voice sounded strange and uncanny in her ears.

For what seemed a long time there was no other sound than the gently moving leaves about her, the birds and the heavy breathing of Baldy. Then, from the brush behind her, came another voice. It came from the direction of the trail down which she had ridden. She realized that she must have passed within a few feet of the man who now spoke.

"What do you want?"

"I have come to warn you. You are being watched."

"You mean you are not alone? There are others with you? Then tell them to go away, for we have our rifles. We have done nothing. We're tending our bees —they're just below the ridge above our camp."

"There is no one with me. I do not mean that others are watching you now, but that others know that you come down out of the hills with something each Friday night, and they want to find out what it is you bring."

There was a rustling in the brush behind her, and she turned to see a man emerge, carrying a rifle ready in his hands. He was a Mexican, swarthy and ill-favored, his face pitted by smallpox. Almost immediately two other men stepped from the brush at other points about the camp. The three walked to where Shannon sat upon her mount. All were armed, and all were Mexicans.

"What do you know about what we bring out of the hills? Should we not bring our honey out?" asked the pock-marked one.

"I know what you bring out," she said. "I am not going to expose you. I am here to warn you."

"Why?"

"I know Allen."

Immediately their attitude changed. "You have seen Allen? You bring a message from him?"

"I have not seen him. I bring no message from him; but for reasons of my own I have come to warn you not to bring down another load next Friday night."

CHAPTER XX

The pock-marked Mexican stepped close to Shannon and took hold of her bridle reins.

"You think," he said in broken English, "we are damn fool? If you do not come from Allen, you come for no good to us. You tell us the truth, damn quick, or you never go back to tell where you find us and bring policemen here!"

His tone was ugly and his manner threatening.

"I have come to warn you because a friend of mine is going to watch for you next Friday night. He does not know who you are, or what you bring out of the hills. I do, and so I know that rather than be caught you might kill him, and I do not want him killed. That is all."

"How do you know what we bring out of the hills?"

"Allen told me."

"Allen told you? I do not believe you. Do you know where Allen is?"

"He is in jail in Los Angeles. I heard him telling a man in Los Angeles last July."

"Who is the friend of yours that is going to watch for us?"

"Mr. Pennington."

"You have told him about us?"

"I have told you that he knows nothing about you. All he knows is that some one comes down with burros from the hills, and that they cut his fence last Friday night. He wants to catch you and find out what you are doing."

"Why have you not told him?"

She hesitated.

"That can make no difference," she said presently.

"It makes a difference to us. I told you to tell the truth, or —"

The Mexican raised his rifle that she might guess the rest.

"I did not want to have to explain how I knew about you. I did not want Mr. Pennington to know that I knew such men as Allen."

"How did you know Allen?"

"That has nothing to do with it at all. I have warned you so that you can take steps to avoid discovery and capture. I shall tell no one else about you. Now let me go."

She gathered Baldy and tried to rein him about, but the man clung to her bridle.

"Not so much of a hurry, senorita! Unless I know how Allen told you so much, I cannot believe that he told you anything. The police have many ways of learning things—sometimes they use women. If you are a friend to Allen, all right. If you are not, you know too damn much for to be very good for you health. You had better tell me all the truth, or you shall not ride away from here—ever!"

"Very well," she said. "I met Allen in a house in Hollywood where he sold his 'snow', and I heard him telling the man there how you disposed of the whiskey that was stolen in New York, brought here to the coast in a ship, and hidden in the mountains."

"What is the name of the man in whose house you met Allen?"

"Crumb."

The man raised his heavy brows.

"How long since you been there—in that house in Hollywood?"

"Not since the last of July. I left the house the same time Allen did."

"You know how Allen he get in jail?" the Mexican asked.

The girl saw that a new suspicion had been aroused in the man, and she judged that the safer plan was to be perfectly frank.

"I do not know, for I have neither seen Crumb nor Allen since; but when I read in the paper that he had been arrested that night, I guessed that Crumb had done it. I heard Crumb ask him to deliver some snow to a man in Hollywood. I know that Crumb is a bad man, and that he was trying to steal your share of the money from Allen."

The man thought in silence for several minutes, the lines of his heavy face evidencing the travail with which some new idea was being born. Presently he looked up, the light of cunning gleaming in his evil eyes.

"You go now," he said. "I know you! Allen tell me about you a long time ago. You Crumb's woman, and your name is Gaza. You will not tell anything about us to your rich friends the Penningtons—you bet you won't!"

The Mexican laughed loudly, winking at his companions.

Shannon could feel the burning flush that suffused her face. She closed her eyes in what was almost physical pain, so terrible did the humiliation torture her pride, and then came the nausea of disgust. The man had dropped her reins, and she wheeled Baldy about.

"You will not come Friday night?" she asked, wishing some assurance that her sacrifice had not been entirely unavailing.

"Mr. Pennington will not find us Friday night, and so he will not be shot."

She rode away then; but there was a vague suspicion lurking in her mind that there had been a double meaning in the man's final words.

Custer Pennington, occupied in the office for a couple of hours after lunch, had just come from the house, and was standing on the brow of the hill looking out over the ranch toward the mountains. His gaze, wandering idly at first, was suddenly riveted upon a tiny speck moving downward from the mouth of a distant ravine—a moving speck which he recognized, even at that distance, to be a horseman, where no horseman should have been. For a moment he watched it, and then, returning to the house, he brought out a pair of binoculars. Now they were clearly revealed by the powerful lenses, the horse and its rider—Baldy and Shannon!

After a while he saw her emerge from Horse Camp Canyon and follow the road to her own place. Custer ran his fingers through his hair in perplexity. He was troubled not only because Shannon had ridden without him, after telling him that she could not ride that afternoon, but also because of the direction in which she had ridden—the trail of which he had told her that he thought it led to the solution of the mystery of the nocturnal traffic. He had told her that he would not ride it before Saturday, for fear of arousing the suspicions of the men he wished to surprise in whatever activity they might be engaged upon; and within a few hours she had ridden deliberately into the mountains on that very trail.

The more Custer considered the matter; the more perplexed he became. At last he gave it up in sheer disgust. Doubtless Shannon would tell him all about it when he called for her later in the afternoon. He tried to forget it; but the thing would not be forgotten.

Several times he realized, with surprise, that he was hurt because she had ridden without him. He tried to argue that he was not hurt, that it made no difference to him, that she had a perfect right to ride with or without him as she saw fit, and that he did not care a straw one way or the other.

Yet, argue as he would, the fact remained that it had made a difference, and that he was considering Shannon now in a new light. Just what the change meant he probably could not have satisfactorily explained, had he tried; but he did not try. He knew that there was was a difference, and that his heart ached when it should not ache. It made him angry with himself, with the result that he went to his room and had another drink.

Shannon, too, felt the difference. She thought that it was her own guilty conscience, though why she should feel guilt for having risked so much for his sake she did not know. Instinctively she was honest, and so to deceive one who she loved, even for a good purpose, troubled her.

At dinner that night Eva was unusually quiet until the colonel, noticing it, asked if she was ill.

"There!" she cried. "You all make life miserable for me because I talk too much, and then, when I give you a rest, you ask if I am ill. What shall I do? If I talk, I pain you. If I fail to talk, I pain you; but if you must know, I am too thrilled to talk just now—I am going to be married!"

"All alone?" inquired Custer.

Guy grinned sheepishly, and was about to venture an explanation when Eva interrupted him. The others at the table were watching the two with amused smiles.

"You see, momsy," said Eva, addressing her mother, "Guy has sold a story. He got a thousand dollars for it—a thousand!"

"Oh, not a thousand!" expostulated Guy.

"Well, it was nearly a thousand—if it had been three hundred dollars more it would have been—and so now that our future's assured we are going to be married. I hadn't intended to mention it until Guy had talked with popsy, but this will be very much nicer, and easier for Guy."

They were all laughing now, including Eva and Guy. The tears were rolling down Custer's cheeks.

"That editor was guilty of grand larceny when he offered you seven hundred berries for the story. Why the gem alone is easily worth a thousand. Adieu, Mark Twain! Farewell, Bill Nye! You've got 'em all nailed to the post, Guy Thackeray!"

The colonel wiped his eyes.

"I gather," he said,. "that you two children wish to get married. Do I surmise correctly?"

"Oh, popsy, you're just wonderful!" exclaimed Eva.

"Yes, how did you guess it, father?" asked Custer. "Marvelous deductive faculties for an old gentleman, I'll say!"

"That will be about all from you, Custer," admonished the colonel.

"Any time that I let a chance like this slip!" returned young Pennington. "Do you think I have forgotten how those two imps pestered the life out of Grace and me a few short years ago? Nay, nay!"

"I don't blame Custer a bit," said Mrs. Evans.

"Guy and Eva certainly did make life miserable for him and Grace."

"That part of it is all right—it is Guy's affair and Eva's; but did you hear him refer to me as an old gentleman?"

They all laughed.

"But you are a gentleman," insisted Custer.

The colonel, his eyes twinkling, turned to Mrs. Evans.

"Times have changed, Mae, since we were children. Imagine speaking thus to our fathers!"

"I'm glad they have changed, Custer. It's terrible to see children afraid of their parents. It has driven so many of them away from home."

"No danger of that here," said the colonel.

"It is more likely to be the other way around," suggested Mrs. Pennington. "In the future we may hear of parents leaving home because of the exacting tyranny of their children."

"My children shall be brought up properly," announced Eva, "with proper respect for their elders."

"Guided by the shining example of their mother," said Custer.

"And their Uncle Cutie," she retorted.

"Come now," interrupted the colonel, "let's hear something of your plans. When are you going to be married?"

"Yes," offered Custer. "Now that the seven hundred dollars has assured their future, there is no reason why they shouldn't be married at once and take a suite at the Ambassador. I understand they're as low as thirty-five hundred a month."

"Aw, I have more than the seven hundred," said Guy. "I've been saving up for a long time. We'll have plenty to start with."

Shannon noticed that he flushed just a little as he made the statement, and she alone knew why he flushed. It was too bad that Custer's little sister should start her married life on money of that sort!

Shannon felt that at heart Guy was a good boy—that he must have been led into this traffic without any adequate realization of its criminality. Her own misfortune had made her generously ready to seek excuses for wrongdoing in others; but she dreaded to think what it was going to mean to Eva and the other Penningtons if ever the truth became known. From her knowledge of the sort of men with whom Guy was involved, she was inclined to believe that the menace of exposure or blackmail would hang over him for many years, even if the former did not materialize in the near future; for authorities, they would immediately involve him, and would try to put the full burden of responsibility upon his shoulders.

"I don't want the financial end of matrimony to worry either of you," the colonel was saying. "Guy has chosen a profession in which it may require years of effort to produce substantial returns. All I shall ask of my daughter's husband is that he shall honestly apply himself to his work. If you do your best, Guy, you will succeed, and in the meantime I'll take care of the finances."

CHAPTER XXI

On the following Monday a pock-marked Mexican appeared at the county jail in Los Angeles, during visitor's hours, and asked to see Slick Allen. The two stood in a corner and conversed in whispers. Allen's face wore an ugly scowl when his visitor told him of young Pennington's interference with their plans.

"It's getting too hot for us around there," said Allen. "We got to move. How much junk you got left?"

"About sixty cases of booze. We got rid of nearly three hundred cases on the cast side, without sending 'em through Evans. There isn't much of the other junk left—a couple of pounds altogether, at the outside."

"We got to lose the last of the booze," said Allen; "but we'll get our money's worth out of it. Now you listen, and listen careful, Bartolo."

He proceeded very carefully and explicitly to explain the details of a plan which brought a grin of sinister amusement to the face of the Mexican. It was not an entirely new plan, but rather an elaboration and improvement of one that Allen had conceived some time before in the event of a contingency similar to that which had now arisen.

"And what about the girl?" asked Bartolo. "She should pay well to keep the Pennington's from knowing."

"Leave her to me," replied Allen. "I shall not be in jail forever."

During the ensuing days of that late September week, when Shannon and Custer rode together, there was a certain constraint in their relations that was new and depressing. The girl was apprehensive of the outcome of his adventure on the rapidly approaching Friday, while he could not rid himself of the haunting memory of her solitary and clandestine ride over the mysterious trail that led into the mountains.

At last Friday came. Neither had reverted, since the previous Saturday, to the subject that was uppermost in the minds of each; but now Shannon could not refrain from seeking once more to defer Custer from his project. She had not been able to forget the sinister smile of the Mexican, or to rid her mind of an intuitive conviction that the man's final statement had concealed a hidden threat. They were parting at the fork of the road—she had hesitated until the last moment.

"You still intend to try to catch those men tonight?" she asked.

"Yes—why?"

"I had hoped you would give it up. I am afraid something may happen. I—oh, please don't go, Custer!" She wished that she might add: "For my sake."

He laughed shortly. "I guess there won't be any trouble. If there is, I can take care of myself."

She saw that it was useless to insist further.

"Let me know if everything is all right," she asked. "Light the light in the big cupola on the house when you get back—I can see it from my bedroom window—and then I shall know that nothing has happened. I shall be watching for it."

"All right," Custer promised, and they parted.

When he reached the house, the ranch bookkeeper came to tell him that the Los Angeles operator had been trying to get him all afternoon.

"Somebody in L. A. wants to talk to you on important business," said the bookkeeper. "You're to call back the minute you get here." Five minutes later he had his connection. An unfamiliar voice asked if he were the younger Mr. Pennington.

"I am," he replied.

"Some one cut your fence last Friday. You like to know who he is?"

"What about it? Who are you?"

"Never mind who I am. I was with them. They double-crossed me. You want to catch 'em?"

"I want to know who they are, and why they cut my fence, and what the devil they're up to back there in the hills."

"You listen to me. You sabe Jackknife Canyon?"

"Yes."

"To-night they bring down the load just before dark. They do that every Friday, and hide the burros until very late. Then they come down into the valley while every one is asleep. To-night they hide 'em in Jackknife. They tie 'em there an' go away. About ten o'clock they come back. You be there nine o'clock, and you catch 'em when they come back. Sabe?

"How many of 'em are there?"

"Only two. You don't have to be afraid—they don't pack no guns. You take gun an' you catch 'em all alone."

"But how do I know that. you're not stringing me?"

"You listen. They double-cross me. I get even. You no want to catch 'em, I no care—that's all. Goodbye!"

Custer turned away from the phone, running his fingers through his hair in a characteristic gesture signifying perplexity. What should he do? The message sounded rather fishy, he thought; but it would do no harm to have a look into Jackknife Canyon around nine o'clock. If he was being tricked, the worst he could fear was that they had taken this method of luring him to Jackknife while they brought the loaded burros down from the hills by some other route. If they had done that, it was very clever of them; but he would not be fooled a second time.

Custer Pennington didn't care to be laughed at, and so, if he was going to be hoaxed that night, he had no intention of having a witness to his idiocy. For that reason he did not take Jake with him, but rode alone up Sycamore when all the inmates of the castle on the hill thought him in bed and asleep.

When he turned into Jackknife, he reined the Apache in and sat for a moment listening. From farther up the canyon, out of sight, there came the shadow of a sound. That would be the tethered burros, he thought, if the whole thing was not a trick; but he was certain that he heard the sound of something moving there.

He rode on again, but he took the precaution of loosening his gun in its holster. There was, of course, the bare possibility of a sinister motive behind the message he had received. As he thought of it now, it occurred to him that his informant was perhaps a trifle too insistent in assuring him that it was safe to come up here alone. Well, the man had put it over cleverly, if that had been his intent.

Now Custer saw a dark mass beneath a sycamore. He rode directly toward it, and in another moment he saw that it represented half a dozen laden burros tethered to the tree. He moved the Apache close in to examine them. There was no sign of men about.

He examined the packs, leaning over and feeling one. What they contained he could not guess; but it was not firewood. They evidently consisted of six wooden boxes to each burro, three on a side.

He reined the Apache in behind the burros in the darkness of the tree's shade, and there he waited for the coming of the men. He did not like the look of things at all. What could those boxes contain?

As he sat there waiting, he had ample time to think. He speculated upon the identity and purpose of the mysterious informant who had called him up from Los Angeles. He speculated again upon the contents of the packs. He recalled the whiskey that Guy had sold him from time to time, and wondered if the packs might not contain liquor. He had gathered from Guy that his supply came from Los Angeles, and he had never given the matter a second thought; but now he recalled the fact, and concluded that if this was whiskey, it was not from the same source as Guy's.

Then from the mouth of Jackknife he heard the sound of horses' hoofs. The Apache pricked up his ears, and Custer leaned forward and laid a hand upon his nostrils. "Quiet boy!" he admonished, in a low whisper.

The sounds approached slowly, halting occasionally. Presently two horsemen rode directly past him on the far side of the canyon. They rode at a brisk trot. Apparently they did not see the pack train, or, if they saw it, they paid no attention to it. They disappeared in the darkness, and the sounds of their horses' hoofs ceased. Pennington knew that they had halted. Who could they be? Certainly not the drivers of the pack train, else they would have stopped with the burros.

He listened intently. Presently he heard horses walking slowly toward him from up the canyon. The two who had passed were coming back— stealthily.

"I sure have got myself in a pretty trap!" he soliloquized a moment later, when he heard the movement of mounted men in the canyon below him. He drew his gun and sat waiting. It was not long that he had to wait. A voice coming from a short distance down the canyon addressed him.

"Ride out into the open and hold up your hands!" it said. "We got you surrounded and covered. If you make a break, we'll bore you. Come on, now, step lively—and keep your hands up!"

It was the voice of an American.

"Who in thunder are you?" demanded Pennington.

"I am a United States marshal," was the quick reply.

Pennington laughed. There was something convincing in the very tone of the man's voice—possibly because Custer had been expecting to meet Mexicans. Here was a hoax indeed; but evidently as much on the newcomers as on himself. They had expected to find a lawbreaker. They would doubtless be angry when they discover that they had been duped.

Custer rode slowly out from beneath the tree.

"Hold up your hands, Mr. Pennington!" snapped the marshal.

Custer Pennington was nonplussed. They knew who he was, yet they demanded that he should hold up his hands like a common criminal.

"Hold on there!" he cried. "What's the joke? If you know who I am, what do you want me to hold up my hands for? How do I know you're a marshal?"

"You don't know it; but I know that you're armed, and that you're in a mighty bad hole. I don't know what you might do, and I ain't taking no chances. So stick 'em up, and do it quick. If anybody's going to get bored around here it'll be you, and not none of my men!"

"You're a damned fool," said Pennington succinctly; but he held his hands before his shoulders, as he had been directed. Five men rode from the shadows and surrounded him. One of them dismounted and disarmed him. He lowered his hands and looked about at them.

"Would you mind," he said, "showing me your authority for this, and telling me what in hell it's all about?"

One of the men threw back his coat, revealing a silver shield. "That's my authority," he said; "that, and the goods we got on you."

"What goods?"

"Well, we expect to get 'em when we examine those packs."

"Look here!" said Custer. "You're all wrong. I have nothing to do with that pack train or what it's packing. I came up here to catch the fellows who have been bringing it down through Ganado every Friday night, and who cut our fence last week. I don't know any more about what's in those packs than you do—evidently not as much."

"That's all right, Mr. Pennington. You'll probably get a chance to tell all that to a jury. We been laying for you since last spring. We didn't know it was you until one of your gang squealed; but we knew that stuff was somewhere in the hills above L. A., and we aimed to get it and you sooner or later."

"Me?"

"Well, not you particularly, but whoever was bootlegging it. To tell you the truth, I'm plumb surprised to find who it is. I thought all along it was some gang of cheap greasers; but it don't make no difference who it is to your Uncle Sam."

"You say some one told you it was I?" asked Custer.

"Sure! How else would we know it? It don't pay to double-cross your pals, Mr. Pennington."

"What are you going to do with me?" he asked.

"We're going to take you back to L. A. and get you held to the Federal grand jury."

"To-night?"

"We're going to take you back to-night."

"Can I stop at the house first?"

"No, We got a warrant to search the place, and we're going to leave a couple of my men here to do it the first thing in the morning. I got an idea you ain't the only one around there that knows something about this business."

CHAPTER XXII

They took Custer down to the village of Ganado, where they had left their cars and obtained horses. Here they left the animals, including the Apache, with instructions that he should be returned to the Rancho del Ganado in the morning.

The inhabitants of the village, almost to a man, had grown up in neighborly friendship with the Penningtons. When he from whom the officers had obtained their mounts discovered the identity of the prisoner, his surprise was exceeded only by his anger.

"If I'd known who you was after," he said, "you'd never have got no horses from me. I'd a' hamstrung 'em first! I've known Cus Pennington since he was knee high to a grasshopper, and whatever you took him for he never done it. Wait till the colonel hears of this. You won't have no more job than a jack rabbit!"

The marshal turned threateningly toward the speaker.

"Shut up!" he advised. "If Colonel Pennington hears of this before morning, you'll wish to God you was a jack rabbit, and could get out of the country in two jumps! Now you get what I'm telling you—you're to keep your trap closed until morning. Hear me?"

The officers and their prisoner were in the car ready to start. The marshal pointed a finger at Jim.

"Don't forget what I told you about keeping your mouth shut until morning," he admonished.

They drove off toward Los Angeles. Jim watched them for a moment, as the red tail light diminished in the distance. Then he turned into the office of his feed barn and took the telephone receiver from its hook. "Gimme Ganado No. 1," he said to the sleepy night operator.

It was five minutes before continuous ringing brought the colonel to the extension telephone in his bedroom. He seemed unable to comprehend the meaning of what Jim was trying to tell him, so sure was he that Custer was in bed and asleep in a near-by room; but at last he was half convinced, for he had known Jim for many years, and well knew his stability and his friendship.

He hung up the receiver. While he dressed hastily, he explained to his wife the purport of the message he had just received.

"What are you going to do, Custer? she asked.

"I'm going to Los Angeles, Julia. Unless that marshal's driving a racing car, I'll be waiting for him when he gets there!"

Shortly before breakfast the following morning two officers, armed with a warrant, searched the castle on the hill. In Custer Pennington's closet they found something which seemed to fill them with elation—two full bottles of whiskey and an empty bottle, each bearing a label identical with those on the bottles they had found in the cases borne by the burros. With this evidence and the laden pack train, they started off toward the village.

Shannon Burke had put in an almost sleepless night. For hours she had lain watching the black silhouette of the cupola against the clear sky, waiting for the light which would announce that Custer had returned home in safety: but no light shone to relieve her anxiety.

She was up early in the morning, and in the saddle at the first streak of dawn, riding directly to the stables of the Rancho del Ganado. The stableman was there, saddling the horses while they fed.

"No one has come down yet?" she asked.

"The Apache's gone," he replied. "I don't understand it. He hasn't been in his box all night. I was just thinkin' of goin' up to the house to see if Custer was there. Don't seem likely he'd be ridin' all night, does it."

"No," she said. Her heart was in her mouth. She could scarcely speak. "I'll ride up for you." she managed to say.

Wheeling Baldy, she put him up the steep hill to the house. The iron gate that closed the patio arch at night was still down, so she rode around to the north side of the house and coo-hooed to attract the attention of some one within. Mrs. Pennington followed by Eva, came to the door. Both were fully dressed. When they saw who it was, they came out and told Shannon what had happened.

He was not injured, then. The sudden sense of relief left her weak, and for a moment she did not consider the other danger that confronted him. He was safe! That was all she cared about just then. Later she commenced to realize the gravity of his situation, and the innocent part that she had taken in involving him in the toils of the scheme which her interference must have suggested to those actually responsible for the traffic in stolen liquor, the guilt of which they had now cleverly shifted to the shoulders of an innocent man.

But there was something that she could do. When she turned Baldy down the hill from the Pennington's, she took the road home that led past the Evan's ranch, and, turning in, dismounted and tied Baldy at the fence. Her knock was answered by Mrs. Evans.

"Is Guy here?" asked Shannon. Hearing her voice, Guy came from his room, drawing on his coat. "You're getting as bad as the Pennington's, " he said, laughing. "They have no respect for Christian hours!"

"Something has happened," she said, "that I thought you should know about. Custer was arrested last night by government officers and taken to Los Angeles. He was out on the Apache at the time. No one seems to know where he was arrested, or why; but the supposition is that they found him in the hills, for the man who runs the feed barn in the village—Jim— told the colonel that the officers got horses from him and rode up toward the ranch, and that it was a couple of hours later that they brought Custer back on the Apache. The stablemen just told me that the Apache had not been in his stall all night, and I know—Custer told me not to tell, but it will make no difference now—that he was going up into the hills last night to try to catch the men who have been bringing down loads on burros every Friday night for a long time, and who cut his fence last Friday."

She looked straight into Guy's eyes as she spoke; but he dropped his as a flush mounted his cheek.

"I thought,"—she continued, "that Guy might want to go to Los Angeles and see if he could help Custer in any way. The Colonel went last night."

"I'll go now," said Guy. "I guess I can help him."

His voice was suddenly weary, and he turned away with an air of dejection which assured Shannon that he intended to do the only honorable thing that he could do—assume the guilt that had been thrown upon Custer's shoulders, no matter what the consequences to himself. She had little doubt that Guy would do this, for she realized his affection for Custer as well as the impulsive generosity of his nature, which, however marred by weakness, was still fine by instinct.

Half an hour later, after a hasty breakfast, young Evans started for Los Angeles, while his mother and Shannon, standing in the porch of the bungalow, waved their good-byes as his roadster swung through the gate into the county road. Mrs. Evans had only a vague idea as to what her son could do to assist Custer Pennington out of his difficulty; but Shannon Burke knew that Pennington's fate lay in the hands of Guy Evans, unless she chose to tell what she knew.

Colonel Pennington had overtaken the marshal's car before the latter reached Los Angeles, but after a brief parley on the road he had discovered that he could do nothing to alter the officer's determination to place Custer in the county jail pending his preliminary hearing before a United States commissioner. Neither the colonel's plea that his son should be allowed to accompany him to an hotel for the night, nor his assurance that he would be personally responsible for the young man's appearance before the commissioner on the following morning, availed to move the obdurate marshal from his stand; nor would he permit the colonel to talk with the prisoner.

This was the last straw. Colonel Pennington had managed to dissemble outward indications of his rising ire, but now an amused smile lighted his son's face as he realized that his father was upon the verge of an explosion. He caught the older man's eyes and shook his head.

"It'll only make it worse," he cautioned.

The colonel directed a parting glare at the marshal, muttered something about homeopathic intellects, and turned back to his roadster.

CHAPTER XXIII

During the long ride to Los Angeles, and later in his cell in the county jail, Custer Pennington had devoted many hours to seeking an explanation of the motives underlying the plan to involve him in a crime of which he had no knowledge, nor even a suspicion of the identity of its instigators. To his knowledge, he had no enemies whose hostility was sufficiently active to lead them to do him so great a wrong. He had had no trouble with any one recently, other than his altercation with Slick Allen several months before; yet it was obvious that he had been deliberately sacrificed for some ulterior purpose. What that purpose was he could only surmise.

The most logical explanation, he finally decided, was that those actually responsible, realizing that discovery was imminent, had sought to divert suspicion from themselves by fastening it upon another. That they—had selected him as the victim might easily be explained on the ground that his embarrassing interest in their movements had already centered their attention upon him, while it also offered the opportunity for luring him into the trap without arousing his suspicions.

It was, then, just a combination of circumstances that had led him into his present predicament; but there still remained unanswered one question that affected his peace of mind more considerably than all the others combined. Who had divulged to the thieves his plans for the previous night?

Concurrently with that question there arose before his mind's eye a picture of Shannon Burke and Baldy as they topped the summit above Jackknife from the trail that led across the basin meadow back into the hills, he knew not where.

"I can't believe that it was she," he told himself for the hundredth time. "She could not have done it. I won't believe it! She could explain it all if I could ask her; but I can't ask her. There is a great deal that I cannot understand, and the most inexplicable thing is that she could possibly have had any connection whatever with the affair."

When his father came with an attorney, in the morning, the son made no mention of Shannon Burke's ride into the hills, or of her anxiety, when they parted in the afternoon, to learn if he was going to carry out his plan for Friday night.

"Did any one know of your intention to watch for these men?" asked the attorney.

"No one," he replied; "but they might have become suspicious from the fact that the week before I had all the gates padlocked on Friday. They had to cut the fence that night to get through. They probably figured that it was getting too hot for them, and that on the following Friday I would take some other steps to discover them. Then they made sure of it by sending me that message from Los Angeles. Gee, but I bit like a sucker!"

"It is unfortunate," remarked the attorney, "that you had not discussed your plans with some one before you undertook to carry them out on Friday night. If we could thus definitely establish your motive for going alone into the hills, and to the very spot where you were discovered with the pack train, I think it would go much further toward convincing the court that you were there without any criminal intent than your own unsupported testimony to that effect!"

Colonel Pennington snorted.

"The best thing to do now," said the attorney, "is to see if we can get an immediate hearing, and arrange for bail in case he is held to the grand jury."

"I'll go with you," said the colonel.

They had been gone but a short time when Guy Evans was admitted to Custer's cell. The latter looked up and smiled when he saw who his visitor was.

"It was bully of you to come," he said. "Bringing condolences, or looking for material, old thing."

"Don't joke, Cus," exclaimed Evans, "It's too rotten to joke about, and it's all my fault."

"Your fault?"

"I am the guilty one. I've come down to give myself up."

"Just what the devil are you talking about?" inquired Pennington." Do you mean to tell me that you have been mixed up in—well, what do you know about that?" A sudden light had dawned upon Custer's understanding. "That hooch that you've been getting me—that I joked you about—it was really the stuff that was stolen from a bonded warehouse in New York? It wasn't any joke at all?"

"You can see for yourself now how much of a joke it was," replied Evans.

"I'll admit," returned Custer ruefully, "that it does require considerable of a sense of humor to see it in this joint!"

"What do you suppose they'll do to me?" asked Guy. "Do you suppose they'll send me to the penitentiary?"

"Tell me the whole thing from the beginning—who got you into it, and just what you've done. Don't omit a thing, no matter how much it incriminates you. I don't need to tell you, old man, that I'm for you, no matter, what you've done."

"I know that, Cus; but I'm afraid no one can help me. I'm in for it. I knew it was stolen from the start. I have been selling it since last May—seven thousand seven hundred and seventy-six quarts of it—and I made a dollar on every quart. It was what I was going to start housekeeping on. Poor little Eva!" Again a sob half choked him. "It was Slick Allen that started me. First he sold me some; then he got me to sell you a bottle, and bring him the money. Then he had me, or at least he made me think so; and he insisted on my handling it for them out in the valley. It wasn't hard to persuade me, for it looked safe, and it didn't seem like such a rotten thing to do, and

I wanted the money the worst way. I know they're all bum excuses. I shan't make any excuses—I'll take my medicine; but it's when I think of Eva that it hurts. It's only Eva that counts!"

"Yes," said Pennington, laying his hand affectionately on the other's shoulder. "It is only Eva who counts; and because of Eva, and because you and I love her so much, you cannot go to the penitentiary."

"What do you mean—cannot go?"

"Have you told any one else what you have just told me?"

No.

"Don't. Go back home, and keep your mouth shut," said Custer.

"You mean that you will take a chance of going up for what I did? Nothing doing! Do you suppose I'd let you, Cus, the best friend I've got in the world, go to the pen for me— for something I did?"

"It's not for you, Guy. I wouldn't go to the pen for you or any other man; but I'd go to the pen for Eva, and so would you."

"I know it, but I can't let you do it. I'm not rotten, Cus!"

"You've got to—it's the easiest way. We've all got to be punished for what you did—those who love us are always punished for our sins; but let me tell you that I don't think you are going to escape punishment if I go up for this. You're going to suffer more than I. You're going to suffer more than you would if you went up yourself; but it can't be helped. The question is, are you man enough to do this for Eva? It is your sacrifice more than mine."

"My God, Cus, I'd rather go myself!"

"I know you would."

Evans walked slowly from the jail, entered his car, and drove away. Of the two hearts his was the heavier; of the two burdens his the more difficult to bear.

Custer Pennington appearing before a United States commissioner that afternoon for his preliminary hearing, was held to the Federal grand jury, and admitted to bail. The evidence brought by the deputies who had searched the Pennington home, taken in connection with the circumstances surrounding his arrest, seemed to leave the commissioner no alternative. Even the colonel had to admit that to himself, though he would never had admitted it to another. The case would probably come up before the grand jury on the following Wednesday.

That night, at dinner, Custer made light of the charge against him, yet at the same time he prepared them for what might happen, for the proceedings before the commissioner had impressed him with the gravity of his case, as had also the talk he had had with his attorney afterward.

"My boy's word is all I need," replied his mother.

Eva came and put her arms about him.

"They wouldn't send you to jail, would they?" she demanded. "It would break my heart."

"Not if you knew I was innocent."

"N-no, not then, I suppose; but it would be awful. If you were guilty, it would kill me. I'd never want to live if my brother was convicted of a crime, and was guilty of it. I'd kill myself first!"

Her brother drew her face down and kissed her tenderly.

"That would be foolish, dear," he said. "No matter what one of us does, such an act would make it all the worse—for those who were left."

"I can't help it," she said. "It isn't just because I have had the honor of the Penningtons preached to me all my life. It's because it's in me —the Pennington honor. It's a part of me, just as it's a part of you, and mother, and father. It's a part of the price we have to pay for being Penningtons. I have always been proud of it, Custer, even if I am only a silly girl."

"I'm proud of it, too, and I haven't jeopardized it; but even if I had, you mustn't think about killing yourself on my account, or any one's else."

"Well, I know you're not guilty, so I don't have to."

"Good! Let's talk about something pleasant."

"Why didn't you see Grace while you were in Los Angeles?"

"I tried to. I called up her boarding place from the lawyer's office. I understood the woman who answered the phone to say that she would call her, but she came back in a couple of minutes and said that Grace was out on location."

"Did you leave your name?"

"I told the woman who I was when she answered the phone."

"I'm sorry you didn't see her," said Mrs. Pennington. "I often think that Mrs. Evans, or Guy, should run down to Los Angeles occasionally and see Grace."

"That's what Shannon says," said Custer. "I'll try to see her next week, before I come home."

"Shannon was up nearly all afternoon waiting to hear if we received any word from you. When you telephoned that you had been held to the Federal grand jury, she would scarcely believe it. She said there must be some mistake."

"Did she say anything else?"

"She asked whether Guy got there before you were held and I told her that you said Guy visited you in the jail. She seems so worried about the affair—just as if she were one of the family. She is such a dear girl! I think I grow to love her more and more every day."

"Yes," said Custer, non-committally.

"She asked me one rather peculiar question," Eva went on.

"What was that?"

"She asked if I was sure that it was you who had been held to the grand jury."

"That was odd, wasn't it?"

"She's so sure of your innocence just as sure as we are," said Eva.

"Well, that's very nice of her," remarked Custer.

CHAPTER XXIV

The next morning he saw Shannon, who came to ride with them, the Penningtons, as had been her custom. She looked tired, as if she had spent a sleepless night. She had—she had spent two sleepless nights, and she had had to fight the old fight all over again. It had been very hard, even though she had won, for it had shown her that the battle was not over. She had thought that she had conquered the craving; but that had been when she had had no troubles or unhappiness to worry her mind and nerves. The last two days had been days of suffering for her, and the two sleepless nights had induced a nervous condition that begged for the quieting influence of the little white powder.

Custer noticed immediately that something was amiss. The roses were gone from her cheeks, leaving a suggestion of the old pallor; and though she smiled and greeted him happily, he thought that he detected an expression of wistfulness and pain in her face when she was not conscious that others were observing her.

Presently he turned toward her.

"I am going to ride over to the east pasture after breakfast," he said, and waited.

"Is that an invitation?"

He smiled and nodded.

"But not if it isn't perfectly convenient," he added.

"I'd love to come with you. You know I always do."

"Fine! And you'll breakfast with us?"

"Not to-day. I have a couple of letters to write that I want to get off right away; but I'll be up between eight thirty and nine. Is that too late?"

"I'll ride down after breakfast and wait for you—if I won't be in the way."

"I've been thinking." said Eva. "I've been thinking how lonely it will be when you have to go away to jail."

"Why, they can't send me to jail—I haven't done anything," he tried to reassure her.

"I'm so afraid, Cus !" The tears came to her eyes. "I lay awake for hours last night, thinking about it. Oh, Cus, I just couldn't stand it if they sent you to jail! Do you think the men who did it would let you go for something they did? Could any one be so wicked? I never hated any one in my life, but I could hate them, if they don't come forward and save you. I could *hate* them, *hate*hate them! Oh, Cus, I believe that I could *kill* the man who would do such a thing to my brother!"

"Come, dear, don't worry about it. The chances are that they'll free me. Even if they don't, you mustn't feel quite so bitterly against the men who are responsible. There may be reasons that you know nothing of that would keep them silent. Let's not talk about it. All we can do now is to wait and see what the grand jury is going to do. In the meantime I don't intend to worry."

Their ride that morning was over a loved and familiar trail that led across El Camino Corto over low hills into Horse Camp Canyon, and up Horse Camp to Coyote Springs; then over El Camino Largo to Sycamore Canyon and down beneath the old, old sycamores to the ranch. She felt that she knew each bush and tree and boulder, and they held for her the quiet restfulness of the familiar faces of old friends. She should miss them, but she would carry them in her memory forever.

When they came to the fork in the road, she would not let Custer ride home with her.

"At eight thirty, then," he called her, as she urged Baldy into a canter and left them with a gay wave of the hand that gave no token of the heavy sorrow in her heart.

After breakfast, as she was returning to her bungalow to write her letters, she saw a Mexican boy on a bicycle turn in at her gate. They met in front of the bungalow.

"Are you Miss Burke?" he asked. "Bartolo says for you to come to his camp in the mountains this morning, sure," he went on, having received an affirmative reply.

The girl thought for a moment. Possibly here was a way out of her dilemma. If she could force Bartolo by threats of exposure, he might discover a way to clear Custer Pennington without incriminating himself. She turned to the boy.

"Tell him I will come."

"I do not see him again. He is up in his camp now. He told me this yesterday. He also told me to tell you that he would be watching for you, and if you did not come alone you would not find him."

"Very well," she said, and turned into the bungalow.

She wrote her letters, but she was not thinking about them. Then she took them over to Powers to take to the city for her. After that she went to the telephone and called the Rancho del Ganado, asking for Custer when she got the connection.

"I'm terribly disappointed," she said, when he came to the telephone. "I find I simply can't ride this morning; but if you'll put it off until afternoon—"

"Why, certainly! Come up to lunch and we'll ride afterward," he told her.

"You won't go, then, until afternoon?" she asked.

"I'll ride over to the east pasture this morning, and we'll just take a ride any old place that you want to go this afternoon."

"All right," she replied.

She had hoped that he would not ride that morning. There was a chance that he might see her, even though the east pasture was miles from the trail she would ride, for there were high places on both trails, where a horseman would be visible for several miles.

"This noon at lunch, then," he said.

CHAPTER XXV

Half an hour later Custer Pennington swung into the saddle and headed the Apache up Sycamore Canyon.

The trail to the east pasture led through Jackknife. As he passed the spot where he had been arrested on the previous Friday night, the man made a wry face—more at the recollection of the ease with which he had been duped than because of the fact of his arrest.

Below and to Custer's right the ranch buildings lay dotted about in the dust like children's toys upon a gray rug. Beyond was the castle on the hill, shining in the sun, and farther still the soft-carpeted valley, in grays and browns and greens. Then the young man's glance wandered to the left and out over the basin meadow, and instantly the joy died out of his heart and the happiness from his eyes. Straight along the mysterious trail loped a horse and rider toward the mountains, and even at that distance he recognized them as Baldy and Shannon.

This was the end. He was through with her forever. What did he know about her? What did any of them know about her?

She was doubtless a hireling of the gang that had stolen the whiskey and disposed of it through Guy. They had sent her here to spy on Guy and to watch the Penningtons. It was she who had set the trap in which he had been caught, not to save Guy, but to throw the suspicion of guilt upon Custer.

With the realization, the senseless fury of his anger left him. He turned the Apache away, and headed him again toward the east pasture; but deep within his heart was a cold anger that was quite as terrible, though in a different way.

Shannon Burke rode up the trail toward the camp of the smugglers, all unconscious that there looked down upon her from a high ridge behind eyes filled with hate and loathing—the eyes of the man she loved.

As she reached the foot of the trail, she saw Bartolo standing beneath a great oak, awaiting her. His pony stood with trailing reins beneath the tree. A rifle butt protruded from a boot on the right of the saddle. He came forward as she guided Baldy toward the tree.

"Buenos dias, senorita," he greeted her, twisting his pock-marked face into the semblance of a smile.

"What do you want of me?" Shannon demanded.

"I need money," he said. "You get money from Evans. He got all the money from the hooch we take down two weeks ago. We never get no chance to get it from him."

"I'll get you nothing!"

"You get money now—and whenever I want it," said the Mexican, "or I tell about Crumb. You Crumb's woman. I tell how you peddle dope. I know! You do what I tell you, or you go to the pen. Sabe?"

"Now listen to me," said the girl. "I didn't come up here to take orders from you. I came to give you orders."

"What?" exclaimed the Mexican, and then he laughed aloud. "You give me orders? That is damn funny!"

"Yes, it is funny. You will enjoy it immensely when I tell you what you are to do."

"Hurry, then; I have no time to waste." He was still laughing.

"You are going to find some way to clear Mr. Pennington of the charge against him. I don't care what the way is, so long as it does not incriminate any other innocent person. If you can do it without getting yourself in trouble, well and good. I do not care; but you must see that there is evidence before the grand jury next Wednesday that will prove Mr. Pennington's innocence."

"Is that all?" inquired Bartolo, grinning broadly.

"That is all."

"And if I don't it—eh?"

"Then I shall go before the grand jury and tell them about you, and Allen —about the opium and the morphine and the cocaine—how you smuggled the stolen booze from the ship off the coast up into the mountains."

"You think you would do that?" he asked. "But how about me? Wouldn't I be telling everything I know about you? Allen would testify, too, and they would make Crumb come and tell how you lived with him. Oh, no, I guess you don't tell the grand jury nothing!"

"I shall tell them everything. Do you think I care about myself? I will tell them all that Allen and Crumb could tell; and listen, Bartolo—I can tell them something more. There used to be five men in your gang. There were three when I came up last week, and Allen is in jail; but where is the other?"

The man's face went black with anger, and perhaps with fear, too.

"What you know about that?" he demanded sharply.

"Allen told Crumb the first time he came to the Hollywood bungalow that he was having trouble among his gang, that you were a hard lot to handle, and that already one named Bartolo had killed one named Gracial. How would you like me to tell that to the grand jury?"

"You never tell that to no one.'" growled the Mexican. "You know too damn much for your health!"

He had stepped suddenly forward and seized her wrist. She struck at him and at the same time put the spurs to Baldy—in her fear and excitement more severely than she had intended. The high-spirited animal, unused to such treatment, leaped forward past the Mexican, who, clinging to the girl's wrist, dragged her from the saddle. Baldy turned, and feeling himself free, ran for the trail that led toward home.

"You know too damn much!" repeated Bartolo. "You better off up here alongside Gracial!"

The girl had risen to her feet and stood facing him. There was no fear in her eyes. She was very beautiful, and her beauty was not lost upon the Mexican.

"You mean that you would kill me to keep me from telling the truth about you?" she asked.

The man stood facing her, holding her by the wrist. His eyes appraised her boldly.

"You damn good-looking," he said, and pulled the girl toward him. "Before I kill you, I—"

He threw an arm about her roughly, and, leaning far over her as she pulled away, he sought to reach her lips with his.

CHAPTER XXVI

The Apache had taken but a few steps on the trail toward the east pasture when Custer reined him in suddenly and wheeled him about.

"I'll settle this thing now," he muttered. "I'll catch her with them. I'll find out who the others are. By God, I've got her now, and I've got them!"

The cold rage that gripped Pennington brooked no delay. He was glad, though, that he was unarmed; for he knew that when he came face to face with the men with whom Shannon Burke had conspired against him, he might again cease to be master of his anger.

At the summit they met Baldy, head and tail erect, snorting and riderless. The appearance of the horse and his evident fright bespoke something amiss. Custer had seen him just as he was emerging from the upper end of the dim trail leading down the opposite side of the hogback. He turned the Apache into it and headed him down toward the oaks.

Below, Shannon was waging a futile fight against the burly Bartolo. She struck at his face and attempted to push him from her, but he only laughed his crooked laugh and pushed her slowly toward the trampled dust of the abandoned camp.

"Before I kill you—" he repeated again and again, as if it were some huge joke.

He heard the sound of the Apache's hoofs upon the trail above but he thought it was the loose horse of the girl. Custer was almost at the bottom of the trail when the Mexican glanced up and saw him. With a curse, he hurled Shannon aside and leaped toward his pony.

At the same instant the girl saw the Apache and his rider, and in the next she saw Bartolo seize his rifle and attempt to draw it from its boot. Leaping to her feet she sprang toward the Mexican, who was cursing frightfully because the rifle had stuck and he could not readily extricate it from the boot. As she reached him, he succeeded in jerking the weapon free. Swinging about, he threw it to his shoulder and fired at Pennington, just as Shannon threw herself upon him, clutching at his arms and dragging the muzzle of the weapon downward. He struck at her face, and tried to wrench the rifle from her grasp; but she clung to it with all the desperation that the danger confronting the man she loved engendered.

Custer had thrown himself from the saddle and was running toward them. Bartolo saw that he could not regain the rifle in time to use it. He struck the girl a terrible blow in the face that sent her to the ground. Then he turned and vaulted into his saddle, and was away across the bottom and up the trail on the opposite side before Pennington could reach and drag him from his pony.

Custer turned to the girl lying motionless upon the ground. He knelt and raised her in his arms. She had fainted, and her face was very white. He looked down into it—the face of the girl he hated. He felt his arms about her, he felt her body against his, and suddenly a look of horror filled his eyes.

He laid her back upon the ground, and stood up. He was trembling violently. As he had held her in his arms, there had swept over him a almost irresistible desire to crush her to him, to cover her eyes and cheeks with kisses, to smother her lips with them—the girl he hated!

A great light had broken upon his mental horizon—a light of understanding that left all his world in the dark shadow of despair. He loved Shannon Burke.

Again he knelt beside her, and very gently he lifted her in his arms until he could support her across one shoulder. Then he whistled to the Apache, who was nibbling the bitter leaves of the live oak. When the horse came to him, he looped the bridle reins about his arm and started on foot up the trail down which he had just ridden, carrying Shannon across his shoulder. At the summit of the ridge he found Baldy grazing upon the sparse, burned grasses of later September.

It was then that Shannon Burke opened her eyes. At first, confused by the rush of returning recollections she thought that it was the Mexican who was carrying her; but an instant later she recognized the whipcord riding breeches and the familiar boots and spurs of the son of Ganado. Then she stirred upon his shoulder.

"I am all right now," she said. "You may put me down. I can walk."

He lowered her to the ground, but he still supported her as they stood facing each other.

"You came just in time," she said. "He was going to kill me."

"I am glad I came," was all that he said.

She noticed how tired and pinched Custer's face looked, as if he had risen from a sick bed after a long period of suffering. He looked older—very much older—and oh, so sad! It wrung her heart; but she did not question him. She was waiting for him to question her, for she knew that he must wonder why she had come here, and what the meaning of the encounter he had witnessed; but he did not ask her anything, beyond inquiring whether she thought she was strong enough to sit her saddle if he helped her mount.

"I shall be all right now," she assured him.

He caught Baldy and assisted her into the saddle. Then he mounted the Apache and led the way along the trail toward home. They were halfway across the basin meadow before either spoke. It was Shannon who broke the silence.

"You must have wondered what I was doing up there," she said, with a backward nod of her head.

"That would not be strange, would it?"

"I will tell you."

"No," he said, "it is bad enough that you went there today and the Saturday before I was arrested. Anything more that you could tell me would only make it worse."

"But I must tell you, Custer." she insisted. "Now that you have learned this much, I can see that your suspicions wrong me more than I deserve. I came here the Saturday before you were arrested to warn them that you were going to watch for them on the following Friday. Though I did not know the men, I knew what sort they were, and that they would kill you the moment they found they that were discovered. It was only to save your life that I came that other time, and this time I came to try to force them to go before the grand jury and clear you of the charge against you; but when I threatened the man, and he found what I knew about him, he said that he would kill me."

"You did not know that I was going to be arrested that night?"

"Oh, Custer, how could you believe that of me?" exclaimed Shannon.

"I came into all this information—about the work of this gang —by accidentally overhearing a conversation in Hollywood, months ago. I know the names of the principals, I know Guy's connection with them. To-day I was trying to keep Guy's name out, too, if that were possible; but he is guilty and you are not. I cannot understand how he could come back from Los Angeles without telling them the truth and removing the suspicion from you."

"I would not let him," said Pennington.

"You would not let him? You would go to the penitentiary for the crime of another?"

"Not for him, but for Eva. Guy and I thrashed it all out. He wanted to give himself up—he almost demanded that I should let him; but it can't be done. Eva must never know."

"But, Custer, you can't go! It wouldn't be fair—it wouldn't be right. I won't let you go! I know enough to clear you, and I shall go before the grand jury on Wednesday and tell all I know."

"No," he said. "You must not. It would involve Guy."

"I won't mention Guy."

"But you will mention others, and they will mention Guy—don't doubt that for a minute." He turned suddenly toward her. "Promise me, Shannon, that you will not go—that you will not mention what you know to a living soul. I would rather go to the pen for twenty years than see Eva's life ruined."

"Perhaps you are right, but it seems to me she would not suffer any more if Guy went than if her brother went. She loves you very much."

"But she will know that I am innocent. If Guy went, she would know that he was guilty." Shannon had no answer to this, and they were silent for a while. "You will help me to keep this from Eva?" he asked. "Yes."

Shannon felt his eyes upon her, and looked up.

"You have been so good to me, Custer, all of you—you can never know how I have valued the friendship of the Penningtons, or what it has meant to me, or how I have striven to deserve it. I would have done anything to repay a part, at least, of what it has done for me. That was what I was trying to do—that is why I wanted to go before the grand jury, no matter what the cost to me; but I failed, and perhaps I have only made it worse. I do not even know that you believe me."

"I believe you, Shannon," he said. "There is much that I do not understand; but I believe that what you did was done in our interests. There is nothing more that any of us can do now but keep still about what we know, for the moment one of those actually responsible is threatened with exposure Guy's name will be divulged— you may rest assured of that. They would be only too glad to shift the responsibility to his shoulders."

"But you will make some effort to defend yourself?"

"I shall simply plead not guilty, and tell the truth about why I was up there when the officers arrested me."

"You will make no other defense?"

"What other defense can I make that would not risk incriminating Guy?" Custer asked her.

She shook her head. It seemed quite hopeless.

CHAPTER XXVII

Federal officers, searching the hills found the camp above Jackknife Canyon. They collected a number of empty bottles bearing labels identical with those found in Custer Pennington's room. That was all they discovered, except that the camp was located on the Pennington property.

On the 12th of October Custer Pennington was found guilty and sentenced to six months in the county jail for having had several hundred dollars' worth of stolen whiskey in his possession. He was neither surprised nor disheartened. His only concern was for the surprised sensibilities of his family, and these—represented at the trial in the person of his father—seemed far from overwhelmed for the colonel was unalterably convinced of his son's innocence.

Eva, who had remained at home with her mother, was more deeply affected than the others, though through a sense of injustice rather than of shame.

"You are taking it much too hard, dear," said her mother. "One would think that our boy was really guilty."

"Oh, if he really were, I should kill myself!"

The only person, other than the officious reformers, to derive any happiness from young Pennington's fate was Slick Allen. He occupied a cell not far from Custer's, and there were occasions when they were thrown together. Several times Allen saw fit to fling gibes at his former employer, much to the amusement of his fellows. They were usually indirect.

One day, as Custer was passing, Allen remarked in a loud tone:

"There's a lot more of these damn fox-trottin' dudes that put on airs, but ain't nothin' but common thieves!"

Pennington turned and faced him.

"You remember what you got the last time you tried calling me names, Allen? Well, don't think for a minute that just because we're in jail I won't hand you the same thing again some day, if you get too funny. The trouble with you, Allen, is that you are laboring under the misapprehension that you are a humorist. You're not, and if I were you I wouldn't make faces at the only man in this jail who knows about you, and Bartolo, and—Gracial. Don't forget Gracial!"

Allen paled, and his eyes closed to two very narrow slits. He made no more observations concerning Pennington; but he devoted much thought to him, trying to arrive at some reasonable explanation of the man's silence, when it was evident that he must have sufficient knowledge of the guilt of others to clear himself of the charge upon which he had been convicted.

One of the first things to do, when he was released from jail, would be to do away with Bartolo. Bartolo disposed of, the other witnesses would join with Allen to lay the guilt upon the departed. Such pleasant thoughts occupied the time and mind of Slick Allen, as did also his plans for paying one Wilson Crumb a little debt he felt due this one-time friend.

Nor was Crumb free from apprehension for the time that would see Allen's jail sentence fulfilled.

He knew enough of Allen's activities to send the man to a Federal prison for a long term, but these matters he could not divulge without equally incriminating himself. There was, however, one little item of Allen's past which might be used against him without signal danger to Crumb, and that was murder of Gracial. It would not be necessary for Crumb to appear in the matter at all. An anonymous letter to the police would suffice.

With natural predilection of the weak for avoiding or delaying the consummation of their intentions, Crumb postponed the writing of this letter of accusation. There was no cause for hurry, he argued, since Allen's time would not expire until the 6th of the following August. Crumb led a lonely life after the departure of Gaza.

That Gaza de Lure had successfully thrown off the fetters into which he had tricked her never for a moment entered his calculations. Finally, however, it was borne in upon him that there was little likelihood of her returning; and so depressing had become the familiar and suggestive furnishings of the Vista del Paso bungalow that he at last gave it up. He took with him, carefully concealed in a trunk, his supply of narcotics—which he did not find so easy to dispose of since the departure of his accomplice.

During the first picture in which Grace Evans had worked with him, Crumb had become more and more impressed with her beauty and the subtle charm of her refinement, which appealed to him by contrast with the ordinary surroundings and personalities of the K. K. S. studio. There was a quiet restfulness about her which soothed his diseased nerves, and after Gaza's desertion he found himself more and more seeking her society. As was his accustomed policy, his attentions were at first so slight, and increased by such barely perceptible degrees, that, taken in connection with his uniform courtesy, they gave the girl no warning of his ultimate purposes.

In much the same manner that he had tricked Gaza de Lure, he tricked Grace Evans into the use of cocaine; and after that the rest was easy. Renting another and less pretentious bungalow on Circle Terrace, he installed the girl there, and transferred the trunk of narcotics to her care, retaining his room at the hotel for himself.

One evening, toward the middle of October, they were dining together at the Winter Garden. Crumb had brought an evening paper on the street, and was glancing through it as they sat waiting for their dinner to be served. Presently he looked up at the girl seated opposite him.

"Didn't you come from Ganado?" he asked.

She nodded affirmatively.

"Why?"

"Here's a guy from there been sent up for bootlegging— fellow by the name of Pennington."

She half closed her eyes, as if in pain.

"I know," she said. "It has been in the newspapers for the last couple of weeks."

"It isn't Pennington who ought to be in jail," he said. "It's your brother."

She looked at him in surprise, and then she laughed.

"You must have been hitting it up strong to-day, Wilson," she said.

"Oh, no, I haven't; but it's funny I never thought of it before. Allen told me a long while ago that a fellow by the name of Evans was handling the hooch for him. He said he got a job from the Penningtons as stable man in order to be near the camp where they had the stuff cached in the hills. He described Evans as a young blood, so I guess there isn't any doubt about it. You have a brother—I've heard you speak of him."

"I don't believe you," she said.

"It don't make any difference whether you believe me or not. I could put your brother in the pen, and they've only got Pennington in the county jail. All they could get on him, according to this article, was having stolen goods in his possession; but your brother was in on the whole proposition. It was hidden in his hay barn. He delivered it to a fellow who came up there every week, ostensibly to get hay, and your brother collected the money. Gosh, they'd send him up for sure if I ever tipped them off to what I know!"

And thus was fashioned the power he used to force her to his will.

CHAPTER XXVIII

Custer's long hours of loneliness had often been occupied with plans against the day of his liberation. That Grace had not seen him or communicated with him since his arrest and conviction had been a source of wonder and hurt to him. He recalled many times the circumstances of the telephone call, with a growing belief that Grace had been there, but had refused to talk with him. Nevertheless, he was determined to see her before he returned to Ganado.

The woman who answered his ring told him that Grace no longer lived there. At first she was loath to give him any information as to the girl's whereabouts; but after some persuasion she gave him a number on Circle Terrace, and in that direction Pennington turned his car.

As he left his car before the bungalow, and approached the building, he could see into the interior through the screen door, for it was a warm day in April, and the inner door was open. As he mounted the few steps leading to the porch, he saw a woman cross the living room, into which the door opened. She moved hurriedly, disappearing through a doorway opposite and closing the door after her. Though he had but a brief glimpse of her in the darkened interior, he knew that it was Grace, so familiar were every line of her figure and every movement of her carriage.

Crossing the living room, Custer rapped on the door through which he had seen Grace go, calling her by name. Receiving no reply, he flung open the door. Facing him was the girl he was engaged to marry.

With her back against the dresser, Grace stood at the opposite end of the room. Her disheveled hair fell about her face, which was overspread with a sickly pallor. Her wild, staring eyes were fixed upon him. Her mouth, drooping at the corners, tremulously depicted a combination of terror and anger. "Grace!" he exclaimed.

She still stood staring at him for a moment before she spoke.

"What do you mean," she demanded at last, "by breaking into my bedroom? Get out! I don't want to see you. I don't want you here!"

He crossed the room and put a hand upon her shoulder.

"You mean that you don't want me here, Grace? That you don't love me?" he asked.

"Love you?" She broke into a disagreeable laugh. "Why you poor rube, I never want to see you again!"

He stood looking at her for a moment longer, and then he turned slowly and walked out of the bungalow and down to his car. When he had gone, the girl threw herself face down upon the bed and burst into uncontrollable sobs. For the moment she had risen triumphant above the clutches of her sordid vice. For that brief moment she had played her part to save the man she loved from greater torture and humiliation in the future—at what a price only she could ever know.

Custer found them waiting for him on the east porch as he drove up to the ranch house.

Eva was the first to reach him. She fairly threw herself upon her brother, laughing and crying in a hysteria of happiness. His mother was smiling through her tears, while the colonel blew his nose violently, remarking that it was "a hell of a time of year to have a damned cold!"

Custer was surprised that Guy and Mrs. Evans had not been of the party that welcomed his return. When he mentioned this, Eva told him that Mrs. Evans thought the Penningtons would want to have him all to themselves for a while, and that their neighbors were coming up after dinner. And it was not until after dinner that he asked after Shannon.

"We have seen very little of her since you left," explained his mother. "She returned Baldy soon after that, and bought the Senator from Mrs. Evans."

"Eva has missed her company very much," said Mrs. Pennington "I was afraid that we might have done something to offend her, but none of us could think what it could have been."

"I thought she was ashamed of us," said Eva.

"Nonsense!" exclaimed the colonel.

"Of course that's nonsense," said Custer. "She knows as well as the rest of you that I was innocent. "

He was thinking how much more surely Shannon knew his innocence than any of them.

During dinner Eva regained her old-time spirit. More than once the tears came to Mrs. Pennington's eyes as she realized that once more their little family was united, and that the pall of sorrow that had outweighed so heavily upon them for the past six months had at last lifted, revealing again the sunshine of the daughter's heart, which had never been the same since their boy had gone away.

"Oh, Cus!" exclaimed Eva. "The most scrumptious thing is going to happen, and I'm so glad that you are going to be here too. They're going to take a picture on Ganado."

Custer turned toward his father with a look of surprise.

"You needn't blame papa," said Eva. "It was all my fault—or, rather, I should say our good fortune is all due to me. You see, papa wasn't going to let them come at first, but the cutest man came up to see him —a nice, snort, fat little man, and he rubbed his hands together and said 'Vell, colonel?' Papa told him that he had never allowed any picture companies on the place; but I happened to be there, and that was all that saved us, for I teased and teased until finally papa said that they could come, provided they didn't take any pictures up around the house. They didn't want to do that, for they're making a Western picture, and they said the scenery at the back of the ranch is just what they want. They're coming up in a few days, and it's going to be perfectly radiant, and maybe I'll get in the pictures!"

"What outfit is it?" asked the son.

"It's a company from the K. K. S., directed by a man by the name of Crumb."

It was after eight o'clock when the Evanses arrived. Mrs. Evans was genuinely affected at seeing Custer again, for she was as fond of him as if he had been her own son. In Guy, Custer discovered a great change. The boy that he had left had become suddenly a man, quiet and reserved, with a shadow of sadness in his expression. His lesson had been a hard one, Custer knew, and the price that he had had to pay for it had left its indelible mark upon his sensitive character.

The first greetings over; Mrs. Evans asked Custer if he had seen Grace before he left Los Angeles.

"I saw her," he said, "and she is not all well. I think Guy should go up there immediately and try to bring her back. I meant to speak to him about it this evening.

CHAPTER XXIX

The six months that had just passed had been months of indecision and sadness for Shannon Burke. Constantly moved by the conviction that she should leave the vicinity of Ganado and the Penningtons, she was held there by a force that she had not the power to overcome.

Never before since she had left her mother's home in the Middle West had she experienced the peace and content and happiness that her little orchard on the highway imparted to her life. The friendship of the Penningtons had meant more to her than anything that had hitherto entered her life; and to be near them, even if she saw them but seldom, constituted a constant bulwark against the assaults of her old enemy, which still occasionally assailed the ramparts of her will.

Never, in the hills, could her mind dwell upon depressing thoughts. Only cheerful reflections were her companions of those hours of solitude. She thought of the love that had come into her life, of the beauty of it, and of all that it had done to make life more worth the living; of the Penningtons and the example of red-blooded cleanliness that they set—decency without prudery; of her little orchard and the saving problems it had brought to occupy her mind and hands; of her horse and her horsemanship, two never-failing sources of of companionship and pleasure which the Penningtons had taught her to love and enjoy.

On the morning after Custer's return, Guy started early for Los Angeles, while Custer— Shannon not having joined them on their morning ride— re-saddled the Apache after breakfast and rode down to her bungalow. He both longed to see her and dreaded the meeting; for, regardless of Grace's attitude and of the repulse she had given him, his honor bound him to her.

Custer had realized, in that brief interview of the day before, that Grace was not herself. What was the cause of her change he could not guess, since he was entirely unacquainted with the symptoms of narcotics. Even had a suspicion of the truth entered his mind, he would have discarded it as a vile slander upon the girl, as he had rejected the involuntary suggestion that she might have been drinking. His position was distressing for a man to whom honor was a fetish, since he knew that he still loved Grace, while at the same time realizing a still greater love for Shannon.

She saw him coming and came down the driveway to meet him, her face radiant with the joy of his return, and with that expression of love that is always patent to all but the object of its concern.

"Oh, Custer!" she cried. "I am so glad that you are home again! It has seemed years and years, rather than months, to all of us."

"I am glad to be home, Shannon. I have missed you, too. I have missed you all—everything—the hills, the valley, every horse and cow and little pig, the clean air, the smell of flowers and sage—all that is Ganado. "

"You like it better than the city?"

"I shall never long for the city again," he said. "Cities are wonderful, of course, with their great buildings, their parks and boulevards, their fine residences, their lawns and gardens. The things that men have accomplished there fill a fellow with admiration; but how pitiful they really are compared with the magnificence that is ours!" He turned and pointed toward the mountains. "Just think of those hills, Shannon, and the infinite, unthinkable power that uplifted such mighty monuments. Think of the countless ages that they have endured, and .then compare with them the puny efforts of man. Compare the range of vision of the city dweller with ours. He can see across the street, and to the top of some tall buildings, which may look imposing; but place it beside one of our hills, and see what becomes of it. Place it in a ravine in the high Sierras, and you would have difficulty in finding it; and you cannot even think of it in connection with a mountain fifteen or twenty thousand feet in height. Any yet the city man patronizes us country people, deploring the necessity that compels us to pursue our circumscribed existence."

"Pity him," laughed Shannon. "He is as narrow as his streets. His ideals can reach no higher than the pall of smoke that hangs over the roofs of his buildings. I am so glad, Custer, that you have given up the idea of leaving the country for the city!"

"I never really intended to," he replied. "I couldn't have left on father's account; but now I can remain on my own as well as his, and with a greater degree of contentment. You see that my recent experience was a blessing in disguise."

"I am glad if some good came out of it; but it was a wicked injustice, and there were others as innocent as you who suffered fully as much—Eva especially."

"I know," he said. "She has been very lonely since I left, with Grace away, too; and they tell me that you have constantly avoided them. Why? I cannot understand it."

He had dismounted and tied the Apache, and they were walking toward the porch. She stopped, and turned to look at Custer squarely in the eyes.

"How could I have done otherwise?" she asked.

"I do not understand," he replied.

She could not hold her eyes to his as she explained, but looked down, her expression changing from happiness to one of shame and sadness.

"I am sorry, Custer. I would not hurt them. I love them all; but I thought I was doing the thing that you wished. There was so much that you did not understand—that you can never understand—and you were away where you couldn't know what was going on; so it seemed disloyal to do the thing I thought you would rather I didn't do."

"It's all over now," he said. "Let's start over again, forgetting all that has happened in the last six months and a half."

Again, as his hand lay upon her arm, he was seized with an almost uncontrollable desire to crush her to him. Two things deterred him— his loyalty to Grace, and the belief that his love would be unwelcome to Shannon.

CHAPTER XXX

Guy Evans swept over the broad smooth highway at a rate that would have won him ten days in the jail at Santa Ana had his course led him through that village. The impression that Custer's words had implanted in his mind was that Grace was ill, for Pennington had not gone into the details of his unhappy interview with the girl, choosing to leave to her brother a realization of her changed condition, which would have been incredible to him even from the lips of so trusted a friend as Custer.

And so it was that when he approached the bungalow on Circle Terrace, and saw a coupe standing at the curb, he guessed what it portended; for though there were doubtless hundreds of similar cars in the city, there was that about this one which suggested the profession of its owner.

There was no response to his ring, and as the inner door was open he entered. A door on the opposite side of the living room was ajar. As Guy approached it, a man appeared in the doorway, and beyond him the visitor could see Grace lying, very white and still, upon a bed.

"Who are you—this woman's husband?" demanded the man in curt tones. "I am her brother. What is the matter? Is she very ill?"

"Did you know of her condition?"

"I heard last night that she was not well, and I hurried up here. I live in the country. Who are you? What has happened? She is not—my God, she is not—"

"Not yet. Perhaps we can save her. I am a doctor. I was called by a Japanese, who said that he was a servant here. He must have left after he called me, for I have not seen him. Her condition is serious, and requires an immediate operation—an operation of such a nature that I must learn the name of her own physician and have him present. Where is her husband?"

"Husband! My sister is not—" Guy ceased speaking, and went suddenly white. "My God, doctor, you don't mean that she—that my sister —Oh no, not that!"

"She had a fall night before last, and an immediate operation is imperative. Her condition is such that we cannot even take the risk of removing her to a hospital. I have my instruments in my car, but I should have help. Who is her doctor?"

"I do not know."

"I'll get some one. I have given her something to quiet her."

The doctor stepped to the telephone and gave a number. Evans entered the room where his sister lay. She was moving about restlessly and moaning, though it was evident that she was still unconscious.

Changed! Guy wondered that he had known her at all, now that he was closer to her. Her face was pinched and drawn. Her beauty was gone—every vestige of it. She looked old and tired and haggard, and there were terrible lines upon her face that stilled her brother's heart and brought the tears to his eyes.

He heard the doctor summoning an assistant and directing him to bring ether. Then he heard him go out of the house by the front door— to get his instruments, doubtless. The brother knelt by the girl's bed.

"Grace!" he whispered, and threw an arm about her.

Her lids fluttered, and she opened her eyes.

"Guy!"

She recognized him—she was conscious.

"Who did this?" he demanded. "What is his name?"

She shook her head.

"What is the use?" she asked. "It is done."

"Tell me!"

"You would kill him—and be punished. It would only make it worse —for you and mother. Let it die with me!"

"You are not going to die. Tell me, who is he? Do you love him?"

"I hate him!"

"How were you injured?"

"He threw me—against a table."

Her voice was growing weaker. Choking back tears of grief and anger, the young man rose and stood beside her.

"Grace, I command you to tell me!"

Her eyes moved to something beyond the foot of the bed, back to his, and back again to whatever she had been looking at, as if she sought to direct his attention to something in that part of the room. He followed the direction of her gaze. There was a dressing table there, and on it a photograph of a man in a silver frame. Guy stepped to the table and picked up the picture.

"This is he?" His eyes demanded an answer. Her lips moved soundlessly, and weakly she nodded an affirmative. "What is his name?"

She was too weak to answer him. She gasped, and her breath came flutteringly. The brother threw himself upon his knees beside the bed, and took her in his arms. His tears mingled with his kisses on her cheek. The doctor came then and drew him away.

"She is dead!" said the boy, turning away and covering his face with his hands.

"No," said the doctor, after a brief examination. "She is not dead. Get into the kitchen, and get some water to boiling. I'll be getting things ready in here. Another doctor will be here in a few minutes."

A moment later the doctor came in. He had removed his coat and vest and rolled up his sleeves. He placed his instruments in the pan of water on the stove, and then he went to the sink and washed his hands. While he scrubbed, he talked. He was an efficient-looking, businesslike person, and he inspired Guy with confidence and hope.

"She has a fighting chance," he said. "I've seen worse cases pull through. She's had a bad time, though. She must have been lying here for pretty close to twenty-four hours without any attention. I found her fully dressed on her bed— fully dressed except for what clothes she's torn off in pain. If some one had called a doctor yesterday at this time, it might have been all right. It may be all right even now. We'll do the best we can."

The bell rang.

"That's the doctor. Let him in, please."

Guy went to the door and admitted the second physician, who removed his coat and vest and went directly to the kitchen. The first doctor was entering the room where Grace lay. He turned and spoke to his colleague, greeting him; then he disappeared within the adjoining room. The second doctor busied himself about the sink sterilizing his hands. Guy lighted another burner and put on another vessel with water in it.

A moment later the first doctor returned to the kitchen.

"It will not be necessary to operate, doctor," he said. "We were too late!"

His tone and manner were still very businesslike and efficient, but there was an expression of compassion in his eyes as he crossed the room and put his arm about Guy's shoulders.

"Come into the other room, my boy. I want to talk to you," he said.

Guy, dry-eyed, and walking as one in a trance, accompanied him to the little living room.

"You have had a hard blow," said the doctor. "What I am going to tell you may make it harder; but if she had been my sister I should have wanted to know about it. She is better off. The chances are that she didn't want to live. She certainly made no fight for life—not since I was called."

"Why should she want to die?" Guy asked dully. "We would have forgiven her. No one would have ever known about it but me."

"There was something else— she was a drug addict. That was probably the reason why she didn't want to live. The morphine I had to give her to quiet her would have killed three ordinary men."

And so Guy Evans came to know the terrible fate that had robbed his sister of her dreams, of her ambition, and finally of her life. He placed the full responsibility upon the man whose picture had stood in its silver frame upon the girl's dressing table. As he knelt beside the dead girl, he swore to search until he had learned the identity of that man, and found him, and forced from him the only expiation that could satisfy the honor of a brother.

CHAPTER XXXI

The death of Grace had, of course, its naturally depressing effect upon the circle of relatives and friends at Ganado; but her absence of more than a year, the infrequency of her letters, and the fact that they had already come to feel that she was lost to them, mitigated to some degree the keenness of their grief and lessened its outward manifestations. It was Guy who suffered most, for hugged to his breast was the gnawing secret of the truth of his sister's life and death. He had told them that Grace had died of pneumonia, and they had not gone behind his assertion to search the records for the truth.

He did not, however, give up his search. He went often to Hollywood, where he haunted public places and the entrance to studios, in the hope that some day he would find the man he sought; but as the passing months brought no success, and the duties of his ranch and his literary work demanded more and more of his time, he was gradually compelled to push the furtherance of his vengeance into the background, though without any lessening of his determination to compass it eventually.

To Custer, the direct effect of Grace's death was to revive the habit of drinking more than was good for him—a habit from which he had drifted away during the past year. That it had ever been a habit he would, of course, have been the last to admit. He was one of those men who could drink, or leave it alone. The world is full of them, and so are the cemeteries.

Shannon recognized the change in Custer. She attributed it to his grief, and to his increased drinking, which she had sensed almost immediately, as love does sense the slightest change in its object, however little apparent to another. She did not realize that he was purposely avoiding her. She was more than ever with Eva now, for Guy, having settled down to the serious occupations of man's estate, no longer had so much leisure to devote to play.

She still occasionally rode at night, for the daytime rides with Custer were less frequent now. Much of his time was occupied closer in around the ranch, with the conditioning of the show herds for the coming autumn— an activity which gave him a plausible excuse for foregoing his rides with Shannon.

May, June, and July had come and gone—it was August again. Guy's futile visits to Los Angeles were now infrequent. The life of Ganado had again assumed the cheerfulness of the past. The youth of the foothills and valley, reinforced by week-end visitors from the city, filled the old house with laughter and happiness. Shannon was always of these parties, for they would not let her remain away.

It was upon the occasion of one of them, early in August, that Eva announced the date of her wedding to Guy.

"The 2nd of September," she told them. "It comes on a Saturday. We're going to motor to—."

"Hold on!" cautioned Guy. "That's a secret!"

"And when we come back we're going to start building on Hill Thirteen."

"That's a cow pasture,'" said Custer.

"Well, it won't be one any more. You must find another cow pasture."

"Certainly, little one," replied her brother. "We'll bring the cows up here in the ballroom. With five thousand acres to pick from, you can't find a bungalow site anywhere except in the best dairy cow pasture on Ganado!"

"Put on a fox trot, some one," cried Guy. "Dance with your sister, Cus, and you'll let her build bungalows all over Ganado. No one can refuse her anything when they dance with her."

It was later in the evening, after a dance, that Shannon and Custer walked out on the driveway along the north side of the ballroom, and stood looking out over the moon-enchanted valley—a vista of loveliness glimpsed between masses of feathery foliage in an opening through the trees on the hillside just below them. They looked out across the acacias and cedars of lower hill toward the lights of a little village twinkling between two dome-like hills at the upper end of the valley. It was an unusually warm evening, almost too warm to dance.

"I think we'd get a little of the ocean breeze," said Custer, "if we were on the other side of the hill. Let's walk over to the water gardens. There is usually a breeze there, but the building cuts us off from it here."

Side by side, in silence, they walked around the front of the building and along the south drive to the steps leading down through the water gardens to the stables. The steps were narrow and Custer went ahead—which is always the custom of men in countries where there are rattlesnakes.

As Shannon stepped from the cement steps to the gravel walk above the first pool, her foot came down upon a round stone, turning her ankle and throwing her against Custer. For support she grasped his arm. Upon such insignificant trifles may the fate of lives depend. It might have been a lizard, a toad, a mouse, or even a rattlesnake that precipitated the moment which, for countless eons, creation had been preparing; but it was none of these. It was just a little round pebble—and it threw Shannon Burke against Custer Pennington, causing her to seize his arm. He felt the contact of those fingers, and the warmth of her body, and her cheek near his shoulder. He threw an arm about her to support her. Almost instantly she had regained her footing. Laughingly she drew away. "I stepped on a stone," she said in explanation; "but I didn't hurt my ankle."

But still he kept his arm about her. At first Shannon did not understand, and, supposing that he still thought her unable to stand alone, she again explained that she was unhurt.

He stood looking down into her face, which was turned up to his. The moon, almost full, revealed her features as clearly as sunlight—how beautiful they were, and how close. She had not yet fully realized the significance of his attitude when he suddenly threw his other arm about her and crushed her to him; and then before she could prevent, he had bent his lips to hers and kissed her full upon the mouth.

With a startled cry she pushed him away.

"Custer!" she said. "What have you done? This is not like you. I do not understand!"

She was really terrified—terrified at the thought that he might have kissed her without love—terrified that he might have kissed her with love. She did not know which would be the greater catastrophe.

"I couldn't help it, Shannon," he said. "Blame the pebble, blame the moonlight, blame me—it won't make any difference. I couldn't help it; that is all there is to it. I've fought against it for months. I knew you didn't love me; but, oh, Shannon, I love you! I had to tell you."

He had not let her go. They still stood there—his arms about her. "Please don't be angry. Shannon," he begged. "You may not want my love, but there's no disgrace in it. Maybe I shouldn't have kissed you, but I couldn't help it, and I'm glad I did. I have that to remember as long as I live. Please don't be angry!"

She closed her eyes and turned away her head, and for just an instant she dreamed her beautiful dream. Why not? Why not? There could be no better wife than she, for there could be no greater love than hers. He noticed that she no longer drew away. There had been no look of anger in her eyes—only startled questioning; and her face was still so near. Again his arms closed about her, and again his lips found hers.

This time she did not deny him. She was only human— only a woman —and her love, growing steadily in power for many months, had suddenly burst forth in a consuming fire beneath his burning kisses. He felt her lips move in a fluttering sob beneath his, and then then her dear arms stole up about his neck and pressed him closer in complete surrender.

"Shannon! You love me?"

"Ah, dear boy, always!" He drew her to the lower end of a pool, where a rustic seat stood half concealed by the foliage of a drooping umbrella tree.

They did not know how long they had sat there—to them it seemed but a moment—when they heard voices calling their names from above.

"Shannon! Custer! Where are you?" It was Eva calling.

"I suppose we'll have to go," he said. "Just one more kiss!"

He took a dozen; and then they rose and walked up the steps to the south drive.

"Shall I tell them?" he asked.

"Not yet, please."

She was not sure that it would last. Such happiness was too sweet to endure.

Eva spied them.

"Where in the world have you two been?" she demanded. "We've been hunting all over for you, and shouting until I'm hoarse."

"We've been right down there by the upper pool, trying to cool off," replied Custer. "It's too beastly hot to dance."

Eva came closer. "Shannon, you'd better go and straighten your hair before any one else sees you." She laughed and pinched the other's arm. "I'd love it," she whispered in Shannon's ear, "if it were true! You'll tell me, won't you?"

"If it ever comes true, dear"— Shannon returned the whisper— "you shall be the first to know about it."

"Scrumptious! But say, I've got the divinest news—what do you think? Popsy has known it all day and never mentioned it—forgot all about it, he said, until just before he and mother trotted off to bed. Why, the K.K.S. company is coming on Monday, and Wilson Crumb is coming with them!"

Shannon staggered almost as from the force of a physical blow. Wilson Crumb coming! Coming to Ganado! Short indeed had been her sweet happiness!

"What's the matter, Shannon?" asked Custer solicitously. The girl steadied herself quickly.

"Oh, it's nothing," she said, with a nervous laugh. "I just felt a little dizzy for a moment."

CHAPTER XXXII

After Custer left her, Shannon entered the bungalow and sat for a long time before the table on which stood a framed photograph of her mother. Never before had she felt the need of loving counsel so sorely as now. In almost any other emergency she could have gone to Mrs. Pennington, but in this she dared not.

Her only hope lay in avoiding discovery by Wilson Crumb during his stay at Ganado. Her love, and the weakness it had induced, permitted her to accept the happiness from which an unkind fate had hitherto debarred her, and to which even now her honor told her she had no right.

She wished that Custer had not loved her, and that she might have continued to live the life that she had learned to love, where she might be near him, and might constantly see him in the happy consociation of friendship; but with his arms about her and his kisses on her lips she had not had the strength to deny him, or to dissimulate the great love which had ordered her very existence for many months.

In the brief moments of bliss that had followed the avowal of his love, she had permitted herself to drift without thought of the future; but now that the sudden knowledge of the approaching arrival of Crumb had startled her into recollection of the past and consideration of its bearings upon the future, she realized only too poignantly that the demands of honor required that sooner or later she herself must tell Custer the whole sordid story of those hideous months in Hollywood. There was no other way. She could not mate with a man unless she could match her honor with his. There was no alternative other than to go away forever.

It was midnight before she arose and went to her room. She went deliberately to a drawer which she kept locked, and, finding the key, she opened it. From it she took the little black case, and, turning back the cover, she revealed the phials, the needles, and the tiny syringe that had played so sinister a part in her past.

With almost fanatical savagery she destroyed it, crushing the glass phials and the syringe beneath her heel and tearing the little case to shreds. Then, gathering up the fragments, she carried them to the fireplace in the living room and burned them.

On the following day the horses and several loads of properties from the K.K.S. studio arrived at Ganado, and the men who accompanied them pitched their camp well up in Jackknife Canyon. Eva was very much excited, and spent much of her time on horseback, watching their preparations. She tried to get Shannon to accompany her, but the latter found various excuses to remain away, being fearful that even though Crumb had not yet arrived, there might be other employees of the studio who would recognize her.

Crumb and the rest of the company came in the afternoon, although they had not been expected until the following day. Eva, who had made Custer ride up again with her in the afternoon, recalled to the actor-director the occasion upon which she had met him, and they had danced together, some year and a half before.

As soon as he met her, Crumb was struck by her beauty, youth, and freshness. He saw in her a possible means of relieving the tedium of his several weeks' enforced absence from Hollywood— though in the big brother he realized a possible obstacle, unless he were able to carry on his purposed gallantries clandestinely.

In the course of conversation he took occasion to remark that Eva ought to photograph well. "I'll let them take a hundred feet of you," he said, "some day when you're up here while we're working. We might discover an unsung Pickford up here among the hills!"

"She will remain unsung, then," said Custer curtly. "My sister has no desire to go into pictures."

"How do you know I haven't?" asked Eva.

"After Grace?" he asked significantly.

She turned to Crumb.

"I'm afraid I wouldn't make much of an actress," she said; "but it would be perfectly radiant to see myself in pictures just once!"

"Good!" he replied. "We'll get you all right some day that you're up here. I promise your brother that I won't try to persuade you into pictures."

"I hope not," said Custer.

As he and Eva rode back toward the house, he turned to the girl.

"I don't like that fellow Crumb," he said.

"Oh, you're prejudiced! I'll bet anything he's just perfectly lovely!"

Next morning, finding no one with the leisure or inclination to ride with her, Eva rode up again to the camp. They had already commenced shooting. Although Crumb was busy, he courteously took the time to explain the scene on which they were working, and many of the technical details of picture making. He asked her to stay and lunch with them. When she insisted that she must return home, he begged her to come again in the afternoon. Although she would have been glad to do so, for she found the work that they were doing novel and interesting, she declined his invitation, as she already had made arrangements for the afternoon.

He followed her to her horse, and walked beside her down the road a short distance from the others.

"If you can't come down this afternoon," he said, "possibly you can come up this evening. We are going to take some night pictures. I hadn't intended inviting any one, because the work is going to be rather difficult and dangerous, and an audience might distract the attention of the actors; but if you think you could get away alone, I should be very glad to have you come up for a few minutes about nine o'clock. We shall be working in the same place. Don't forget," he repeated, as she started to ride away, "that for this particular scene I really ought to not have any audience at all; so if you come, please don't tell any one else about it."

"I'll come," she said. "It's awfully good of you to ask me, and I won't tell a soul."

Crumb smiled as he turned back to his waiting company.

After lunch that day Custer went to his room, and, throwing himself on his bed with a book, with the intention of reading for half an hour, fell asleep.

Shortly afterward Shannon Burke, feeling that there would be no danger of meeting any of the K.K.S. people at the Pennington house, rode up on the Senator to keep her appointment with Eva. As she tied her horse upon the north side of the house, Wilson Crumb stopped his car opposite the patio at the south drive. He had come up to see Colonel Pennington for the purpose of arranging for the use of a number of the Ganado Herefords in a scene on the following day. Not finding Eva in the family sitting room, Shannon passed through the house and out into the patio, just as Wilson Crumb mounted the two steps to the arcade. Before either realized the presence of the other they were face to face, scarce a yard apart.

Shannon went deathly white as she recognized the man beneath his make-up, while Crumb stood speechless for a moment. "My God, Gaza. You!" he presently managed to exclaim. "What are you doing here? Thank God I have found you at last!"

"Don't!" she begged. "Please don't speak to me. I am living a decent life here."

He laughed in a disagreeable manner.

"Decent!" he scoffed. "Where are you getting the snow? Who's putting up for it?"

"I don't use it any more," she said.

"The hell you don't! You can't put that over on me! Some other guy is furnishing it. I know you—you can't get along two hours without it. I'm not going to stand for this. There isn't any guy going to steal my girl!"

"Hush, Wilson!" she cautioned. "For God's sake keep still! Some one might hear you."

"I don't give a damn who hears me. I'm here to tell the world that no one is going to take my girl away from me. I've found you, and you're going back with me, do you understand?"

She came very close to him, her eyes blazing wrathfully.

"I'm not going back with you, Wilson Crumb," she said. "If you tell, or if you ever threaten me again in any way, I'll kill you. I managed to escape you, and I have found happiness at last, and no one shall take it away from me!"

"What about my happiness? You lived with me two years. I love you, and, by God, I'm going to have you, if I have to—" A door slammed behind them and they both turned to see Custer Pennington standing in the arcade outside his door, looking at them. "I beg your pardon," he said, his voice chilling. "Did I interrupt?"

"This man is looking for some one, Custer," said Shannon, and turned to re-enter the house.

Confronted by a man, Crumb's bravado had vanished. Intuitively he guessed that he was looking at the man who had stolen Gaza from him; but he was a very big young man, with broad shoulders and muscles that his flannel shirt and riding breeches did not conceal. Crumb decided that if he was going to have trouble with this man, it would be safer to commence hostilities at a time when the other was not looking.

"Yes," he said. "I was looking for your father, Mr. Pennington."

"Father is not here. He has driven over to the village. What do you want?"

"I wanted to see if I could arrange for the use of some of your Herefords to-morrow morning."

"You can find out about that," he said, "or anything else that you may wish to know, from the assistant foreman, whom you will usually find up at the other end, around the cabin. If he is in doubt about anything, he will consult with us personally; so that it will not be necessary, Mr. Crumb, for you to go to the trouble of coming to the house again."

Custer's voice was level and low. It carried no suggestion of anger, yet there was that about it which convinced Crumb that he was fortunate in not having been kicked off the hill physically rather than verbally—for kicked off he had been, and advised to stay off, into the bargain.

He wondered how much Pennington had overheard of his conversation with Gaza. Shannon Burke, crouching in a big chair in the sitting room, was wondering the same thing.

As a matter of fact, Custer had overheard practically all of the conversation. The noise of Crumb's car had awakened him, but almost immediately he had fallen into a doze, through which the spoken words impinged upon his consciousness without any actual, immediate realization of their meaning, of the identity of the speakers'. The moment that he became fully awake, and found that he was listening to a conversation not intended for his ears, he had risen and gone into the patio.

When finally he came into the sitting room, where Shannon was, he made no mention of the occurrence, except to say that the visitor had wanted to see his father. It did not seem possible to Shannon that he could have failed to overhear at least a part of their conversation, for they were standing not more than a couple of yards from the open window of his bedroom, and there was no other sound breaking the stillness of the August noon. She was sure that he had heard, and yet his manner indicated that he had not.

She waited a moment to see if he would be the first to broach the subject, but he did not. She determined to tell him then and there all that she had to tell, freeing her soul and her conscience of their burden, whatever the cost might be.

She rose and came to where he was standing, and, placing a hand upon his arm, looked up into his eyes.

"Custer," she said. "I have something to tell you. I ought to have told you before, but I have been afraid. Since last night there is no alternative but to tell you."

"You do not have to tell me anything that you do not want to tell me," he said. "My confidence in you is implicit. I could not both love and distrust at the same time."

"I must tell you," she said. "I only hope—"

"Where in the world have you been, Shannon?" cried Eva, breaking suddenly into the sitting room. "I have been away down to your place looking for you. I thought you were going to play golf with me this afternoon."

"That's what I came up for," said Shannon, turning toward her.

"Well, come on, then! We'll have to hurry, if we're going to play eighteen holes this afternoon."

Custer Pennington went back to his room again after the girls had driven off in the direction of the Country Club. He wondered what it had been that Shannon wished to tell him. Round and round in his mind rang the words of Wilson Crumb:

"You lived with me two years—you lived with me two years— you lived with me two years!"

Custer went to his closet and rummaged around for a bottle. It had been more than two weeks since he had taken a drink. The return to his old intimacy with Shannon, and the frequency with which he now saw her had again weaned him from his habit; but today he felt the need of a drink—of a big drink, stiff and neat.

He swallowed the raw liquor as if it had been so much water. He wished now that he had punched Crumb's head when he had had the chance. The cur! He had spoken to Shannon as if she were a common woman of the streets— Shannon Burke— Custer's Shannon!

Feeling no reaction to the first drink, he took another.

"I'd like to get my fingers on his throat!" he thought. "Before I choked the life out of him, I'd drag him up here and make him kiss the ground at her feet!"

But no, he could not do that. Others would see it, and there would have to be explanations; and how could he explain it without casting reflections on Shannon?

For hours he sat there in his room, nursing his anger, his jealousy, and his grief; and all the time he drank and drank again. He went to his closet, got his belt and holster, and from his dresser drawer took a big, ugly-looking forty-five— a Colt's automatic. For a moment he stood holding it in his hand, looking at it. Almost caressingly he handled it, and then he slipped it into the holster at his hip, put on his hat, and started for the door.

CHAPTER XXXIII

Custer's gait showed no indication of the amount that he had drunk. He was a Pennington of Virginia, and he could carry his liquor like a gentleman. Even though he was aflame with the heat of vengeance, his movements were slow and deliberate. At the door he paused, and, turning, retraced his steps to the table where stood the bottle and the glass. The bottle was empty. He went to the closet and got another. Again he drank, and as he stood there by the table he commenced to plan again.

The colonel and Mrs. Pennington were away somewhere down in the valley. Eva and Shannon were the first to return. In passing along the arcade by Custer's open window, Eva saw him lying on his bed. She called to him, but he did not answer. Shannon was at her side.

"What in the world do you suppose is the matter with Custer?" asked Eva.

They saw that he was fully dressed. His hat had fallen forward over his eyes. The two girls entered the room, when they could not arouse him by calling him from the outside. The two bottles and the glass upon the table told their own story. What they could not tell Shannon guessed—he had overheard the conversation between Wilson Crumb and herself.

Eva removed the bottles and the glass to the closet.

"Poor Cus!" she said. "I never saw him like this before. I wonder what could have happened! What had we better do?"

"Pull down the shades by his bed," said Shannon, and this she did herself without waiting for Eva. "No one can see him from the patio now. It will be just as well to leave him alone. I think, Eva, He will probably be all right when he wakes up."

They went out of the room, closing the door after them, and a little later Shannon mounted the Senator and rode away toward home.

When the colonel and Mrs. Pennington arrived at the ranch house, just before dinner, Eva told them that Custer was not to be disturbed. They did not go to his room at all, and at about half past eight they retired for the night.

Eva was very much excited. She had never before experienced the thrill of such an adventure as she was about to embark upon. As the time approached, she became more and more perturbed. The realization grew upon her that what she was doing might seem highly objectionable to her family; but as her innocent heart held no suggestion of evil, she considered that her only wrong was the infraction of those unwritten laws of well regulated homes which forbid their daughters going out alone at night. She would tell about it in the morning, and wheedle her father into forgiveness.

Quickly she changed into riding clothes. Leaving her room, she noiselessly passed through the living room and the east wing to the kitchen, and from there to the basement, from which a tunnel led beneath the driveway and opened on the hillside above the upper pool of the water gardens. To get her horse and saddle him required but a few moments, for the moon was full and the night almost like day.

As she passed the mouth of Jackknife she glanced up the canyon toward the site of K.K.S. camp, but she could not see any lights, as the camp was fairly well hidden from the main canyon by trees. As she approached El Camino Largo, she saw that all was darkness. There was no sign of the artificial lights she imagined they would use for shooting night scenes, nor was there anything to indicate the presence of the actors.

She continued on, however, until presently she saw the outlines of a car beneath the big sycamore. A man stepped out and hailed her. "Is that you, Miss Pennington?" he asked.

"Yes," she said. "Aren't you going to take the pictures tonight?" She rode up quite close to him. It was Crumb.

"I am just waiting for the others. Won't you dismount?"

As she swung from the saddle, he led her horse to his car and tied him to the spare tire in the rear; then he returned to the girl. As they talked, he adroitly turned the subject of their conversation toward the possibilities for fame and fortune which lay in pictures for a beautiful and talented girl.

So unsophisticated was Eva, and so innocent, that she did not realize from his conversation what would have been palpable to one more worldly wise; and because she did not repulse him, Crumb thought that she was not averse to his advances. It was not until he seized her and tried to kiss her that she awoke to a realization of her danger, and of the position in which her silly credulity had placed her.

She carried a quirt in her hand, and she was a Pennington. "How dare you?" she cried, attempting to jerk away.

When he would have persisted, she raised the heavy quirt and struck him across the face. "My father shall hear of this, and so shall the man I am to marry—Mr. Evans."

"Go slow!" he growled angrily. "Be careful what you tell! Remember that you came up here alone at night to meet a man you have known only a day. How will you square with that your assertions of virtue, eh? And as for Evans—yes, one of your men told me today that you and he were going to be married—as for him, the less you drag him into this the better it'll be for Evans, and you, too!"

She was walking toward her horse. She wheeled suddenly toward him.

"Had I been armed, I would have killed you," she said. "Any Pennington would kill you for what you attempted. My father or my brother will kill you if you are here tomorrow, for I shall tell them what you have done. You had better leave tonight. I am advising you for their sakes—not for yours."

He followed her then, and, when she mounted, he seized her reins. "Not so damned fast, young lady! I've got something to say about this. You'll keep your mouth shut, or I'll send Evans to the pen, where he belongs!"

"Get out of my way!" she commanded, and put her spurs to her mount. The horse leaped forward, but Crumb clung to the reins, checking him. Then she struck Crumb again; but he managed to seize the quirt and hold it.

"Now listen to me," he said. "If you tell what happened here tonight, I'll tell what I know about Evans, and he'll go to the pen as sure as you're a silly little fool!"

"You know nothing about Mr. Evans. You don't even know him."

"Listen—I'll tell you what I know. I know that Evans let your brother, who was innocent, go to the pen for the thing that Evans was guilty of." The girl shrank back.

"You lie!" she cried.

"No, I don't lie, either. I'm telling you the truth, and I can bring plenty of witnesses to prove what I say. It was young Evans who handled all that stolen booze and sold it to some guy from L.A. It was young Evans who got the money. He was getting rich on it till your brother butted in and crabbed his game, and then it was young Evans who kept still and let an innocent man do time for him. That's the kind of fellow you're going to marry. If you want the whole world to know about it, you just tell your father or your brother anything about me!"

He saw the girl sink down in her saddle, her head and shoulders drooping like some lovely flower in the path of fire, and he knew that he had won. Then he let her go.

It was half past nine o'clock when Colonel Pennington was aroused by some one knocking on the north door of his bedroom—the door that opened upon the north porch. "Who is it?" he asked. It was the stableman.

"Miss Eva's horse is out, sir," the man said. "I heard a horse pass the bunk house about half an hour ago. I dressed and come up here to the stables, to see if it was one of ours—somethin' seemed to tell me it was —an' I found her horse out. I thought I'd better tell you about it, sir. You can't tell, sir, with all them picture-people up the canyon, what might be goin' on. We'll be lucky if we have any horses or tack left if they're here long!"

"Miss Eva's in bed," said the colonel. "but we'll have to look into this at once. Custer's sick tonight, so he can't go along with us; but if you will saddle up my horse, and one for yourself, I'll dress and be right down. It can't be the motion-picture people— they're not horse thieves."

While the stableman returned to saddle the horses, the colonel dressed. So sure was he that Eva was in bed that he did not even stop to look into her room. As he left the house, he was buckling on a gun—a thing that he seldom carried, for even in the peaceful days that have settled upon southern California a horse thief is still a horse thief.

As he was descending the steps to the stable, he saw some one coming up. In the moonlight there was no difficulty in recognizing the figure of his daughter.

"Eva!" he exclaimed, "Where have you been? What are you doing out at this time of night, alone?"

She did not answer, but threw herself into his arms, sobbing.

"What is it? What has happened, child? Tell me!"

Her sobs choked her, and she could not speak. Putting his arm about her, her father led her up the steps and to her room. There he sat down and held her, and tried to comfort her. Little by little, word by word, she managed at last to tell him. "You mustn't cry dear," he said. "You did a foolish thing to go up there alone, but you did nothing wrong. As for what that fellow told you about Guy, I don't believe it."

"But it's the truth," she sobbed. "I know it is the truth now. Little things that I didn't think of before come back to me, and in the light of what that terrible man told me I know that it's true. We always knew that Custer was innocent. Think what a change came over Guy from the moment that Custer was arrested. He has been a different man since. And the money— the money that we were to be married on. I never stopped to try to reason it out. He had thousands of dollars. He told me not to tell anybody how much he had; and that was where it came from.

"It couldn't have come from anything else. Oh, popsy, it is awful, and I loved him so! To think that he, that Guy Evans, of all men, would have let my brother go to jail for something he did!" Again her sobs stifled her.

"Crying will do no good," the colonel said, "Go to bed now, and tomorrow we will talk it over. Good night, little girl. Remember, we'll all stick to Guy, no matter what he has done." He kissed her then and left her, but he did not return to his room. Instead, he went down to the stables and saddled his horse, for the stableman, when Eva came in with the missing animal, had put it in its box and returned to the bunk house.

The colonel rode immediately to the sleeping camp in Jackknife Canyon. His calls went unanswered for a time, but presently a sleepy man stuck his head through the flap of a tent. "What do you want?" he asked.

"I am looking for Mr. Crumb. Where is he?"

"I don't know. He went away in his car early in the evening, and hasn't come back. What's the matter, anyway? You're the second fellow that's been looking for him. Oh, you're Colonel Pennington, aren't you? I didn't recognize you. Why, some one was here a little while ago looking for him —a young fellow on horseback. I think it must have been your son. Anything I can do for you?"

"Yes," said the colonel. "In case I don't see Mr. Crumb, you can tell him, or whoever is in charge, that you're to break camp in the morning and be off my property by ten o'clock."

He wheeled his horse and rode down Jackknife Canyon toward Sycamore.

"Well, what the hell!" ejaculated the sleepy man to himself, and withdrew again into his tent.

CHAPTER XXXIV

Shannon Burke, after a restless night, rose early in the morning to ride. She always found that the quiet and peace of the hills acted as a tonic on jangling nerves, and dispelled, at least for the moment, any cloud of unhappiness that might be hovering over her.

The first person to see her that morning was the flunky from the K.K.S. camp who was rustling wood for the cook's morning fire. So interested was he in her rather remarkable occupation that he stood watching her from behind a bush until she was out of sight. As long as he saw her, she rode slowly, dragging at her side a leafy bough, which she moved to and fro, as if sweeping the ground. She constantly looked back, as if to note the effect of her work; and once or twice he saw her go over short stretches of the road a second time, brushing vigorously.

It was quite light by that time, as it was almost five o'clock, and the sun was just rising as she dismounted at the Ganado stables and hurried up the steps toward the house. The iron gate at the patio entrance had not yet been raised, so she went around to the north side of the house and knocked on the colonel's bedroom door.

"Colonel," she cried, "Wilson Crumb has been killed. I rode early this morning, and as I came into Sycamore over El Camino Largo I saw his body lying under the big tree there."

They were both thinking the same thought, which neither dared voice—where was Custer?

"Did you notify the camp?" he asked.

"No—I came directly here."

"You are sure that it is Crumb, and that he is dead?" he asked.

"I am sure that it is Crumb. He was lying on his back, and though I didn't dismount I am quite positive that he was dead."

Mrs. Pennington had joined them, herself dressed for riding. "How terrible!" she exclaimed.

"Terrible nothing," exclaimed the colonel. "I'm damned glad he's dead!"

Shannon looked at him in astonishment, but Mrs. Pennington understood, for the colonel had told her all that Eva had told him.

"He was a bad man," said Shannon. "The world will be better off without him."

"You knew him?" Colonel Pennington asked in surprise. "I knew him in Hollywood," she replied.

She knew now that they must all know sooner or later, for she could not see how she could be kept out of the investigation and the trial that must follow. In her heart she feared that Custer had killed Crumb. The fact that he had drunk so heavily that afternoon indicated not only that he had overheard, but that what he had heard had affected him profoundly—profoundly enough to have suggested the killing of the man whom he believed to have wronged the woman he loved.

"The first thing to do, I suppose," said the colonel, "is to notify the sheriff." He left the room and went to the telephone. While he was away Mrs. Pennington and Shannon discussed the tragedy, and the older woman confided to the other the experience that Eva had had with Crumb the previous night.

"The beast!" muttered Shannon. "Death was too good for him!" Presently the colonel returned to them.

"I think I'll go and see if the children are going to ride with us," he said. "There is no reason why we shouldn't ride as usual."

He went to Eva's door and looked in. Apparently she was still fast asleep. Her hair was down, and her curls lay in soft confusion upon her pillow. Very gently he closed the door again, glad that she could sleep. When he entered his son's room he found Custer lying fully clothed upon his bed, his belt about his waist and his gun at his hip. His suspicions were crystallized into belief. But why had Custer killed Crumb? He couldn't have known of the man's affront to Eva, for she had seen no member of the family but her father, and in him alone had she confided.

He crossed to the bed and shook Custer by the shoulder. The younger man opened his eyes and sat up on the edge of his bed. He looked first at his father and then at himself—at his boots and spurs, and breeches, and the gun about his waist. "What time is it?" he asked.

"Five o'clock."

"I must have fallen asleep. I wish it was dinner time! I'm hungry."

"Dinner time! It's only a matter of a couple of hours to breakfast. It's five o'clock in the morning."

Custer rose to his feet in surprise.

"I must have loaded on more than I knew," he said with a wry smile.

"What do you mean?" asked his father.

"I had a blue streak yesterday afternoon, and I took a few drinks; and here I have slept all the way through to the next morning!"

"You haven't been out of the room since yesterday afternoon?" asked the colonel.

"No, of course not. I thought it was still yesterday afternoon until you told me that it is the next morning," said Custer.

The colonel ran his fingers through his hair.

"I am glad," he said.

Custer didn't know why his father was glad.

"Riding?" he asked.

"Yes."

"I'll be with you in a jiffy. I want to wash up a bit."

He met them at the stables a few minutes later. The effect of the liquor had entirely disappeared. He seemed his normal self again, and not as all like a man who had the blood of a new murder on his soul. He was glad to see Shannon, and squeezed her hand as he passed her horse to get his own.

They were mounted, and had started out, when the colonel reined to Custer's side.

"Shannon just made a gruesome find up in Sycamore," he said, and paused.

If he had intended to surprise Custer into any indication of guilty knowledge, he failed.

"Gruesome find!" repeated the younger man. "What was it?"

"Wilson Crumb has been murdered. Shannon found his body."

"The devil!" ejaculated Custer. "Who do you suppose could have done it?"

Then, quite suddenly, his heart came to his mouth, as he realized that there was only one present there who had cause to kill Wilson Crumb. He did not dare to look at Shannon for a long time.

They had gone only a hundred yards when Custer pulled up the Apache and dismounted.

"I thought so," he said, looking at the horse's off forefoot. "He's pulled that shoe again. He must have done it in the corral, for it was on when I put him in last night. You folks go ahead. I'll go back and saddle Baldy."

The stableman was still there, and helped him.

"That was a new shoe," Custer said. "Look about the corral and the box, and see if you can find it. You can tack it back on." Then he swung to Baldy's back and cantered off after the others.

A deputy sheriff came from the village of Ganado before they returned from their ride, and went up the canyon to take charge of Crumb's body and investigate the scene of the crime.

Eva was still in bed when they called to breakfast. They insisted upon Shannon remaining, and the four were passing along the arcade past Eva's room.

"I think I'll go in and waken her," said Mrs. Pennington. "She doesn't like to sleep so late."

The others passed into the living room, and were walking toward the dining room when they were startled by a scream.

"Custer! Custer!" Mrs. Pennington called to her husband.

All three turned and hastened back to Eva's room, where they found Mrs. Pennington half lying across the bed her body convulsed with sobs. The colonel was the first to reach her, followed by Custer and Shannon. The bedclothes lay half thrown back, where Mrs. Pennington had turned them. The white sheet was stained with blood, and in Eva's hand was clutched a revolver that Custer had given her the previous Christmas.

"My little girl, my little girl!" cried the weeping mother. "Why did you do it?"

The colonel knelt and put his arms about his wife. He could not speak. Custer Pennington stood like a man turned to stone. The shock seemed to have bereft him of the power to understand what had happened. Finally he turned dumbly toward Shannon. The tears were running down her cheeks. Gently she touched his sleeve.

"My poor boy!" she said.

The words broke the spell that had held him. He walked to the opposite side of the bed and bent close to the still, white face of the sister he had worshiped.

"Dear little sister, how could you, when we love you so?" he said.

Gently the colonel drew his wife away, and, kneeling, placed his ear close above Eva's heart. There was no outward indications of life, but presently he lifted his head, and expression of hope relieving that of grim despair which had settled upon his countenance at the first realization of the tragedy.

"She is not dead," he said. "Get Baldwin! Get him at once!" He was addressing Custer. "Then telephone Carruthers, in Los Angeles, to get down here as soon as God will let him."

Custer hurried from the room to carry out his father's instructions.

It was later, while they were waiting for the arrival of the doctor, that the colonel told Custer of Eva's experience with Crumb the previous night.

"She wanted to kill herself because of what he told her about Guy," he said. "There was no other reason."

Then the doctor came, and they all stood in tense expectancy and mingled dread and hope while he made his examination. Carefully and deliberately the old doctor worked, outwardly as calm and unaffected as if he were treating a minor injury to a stranger; yet his heart was as heavy as theirs, for he had brought Eva into the world, and had known and loved her all her brief life.

At last he straightened up, to find their questioning eyes upon him.

"She still lives," he said, but there was no hope in his voice.

"I have sent for Carruthers," said the colonel. "He is on his way now. He told Custer that he'll be here in less than three hours."

"I have arranged to have a couple of nurses sent out, too," said Custer. Dr. Baldwin made no reply.

"There is no hope?" asked the colonel.

"There is always hope while there is life," replied the doctor: "but you must not raise yours too high."

They understood him, and realized that there was very little hope.

"Can you keep her alive until Carruthers arrives?" asked the colonel.

"I need not tell you that I shall do my best," was the reply.

Guy had come, with his mother. He seemed absolutely stunned by the catastrophe that had overwhelmed him. There was a wildness in his demeanor that frightened them all. It was necessary to watch him carefully, for fear that he might attempt to destroy himself when he realized at last that Eva was likely to die.

He insisted that they should tell him all the circumstances that had led up to the pitiful tragedy. For a time they sought to conceal a part of the truth from him; but at last, so great was his insistence, they were compelled to reveal all that they knew.

Of a nervous and excitable temperament, and endowed by nature with a character of extreme sensitiveness and comparatively little strength, the shock of the knowledge that it was his own acts that had led Eva to self-destruction proved too much for Guy's overwrought nerves and brain. So violent did he become that Colonel Pennington and Custer together could scarce restrain him, and it became necessary to send for two of the ranch employees.

When the deputy sheriff came to question them about the murder of Crumb, it was evident that Guy's mind was so greatly affected that he did not understand what was taking place around him. He had sunk into a morose silence broken at intervals by fits of raving. Later in the day, at Dr. Baldwin's suggestion he was removed to a sanatorium outside of Los Angeles.

Guy's mental collapse, and the necessity for constantly restraining him, had resulted in taking Custer's mind from his own grief, at least for the moment; but when he was not thus occupied he sat staring straight ahead of him in dumb despair.

It was eleven o'clock when the best surgeon that Los Angeles could furnish arrived, bringing a nurse with him, and Eva was still breathing when he came. Dr. Baldwin was there, and together the three worked for an hour while the Penningtons and Shannon waited almost hopelessly in the living room, Mrs. Evans having accompanied Guy to Los Angeles.

Finally, after what seemed years, the door of the living room opened, and Dr. Carruthers entered. They scanned his face as he entered, but saw nothing there to lighten the burden of their apprehension. The colonel and Custer rose.

"Well?" asked the former, his voice scarcely audible.

"The operation was successful. I found the bullet and removed it."

"She will live, then!" cried Mrs. Pennington, coming quickly toward him.

He took her hands very gently in his.

"My dear madam," he said, "it would be cruel of me to hold out useless hope. She hasn't more than one chance in a hundred. It is a miracle that she was alive when you found her. Only a splendid constitution, resulting from the life she has led, could possibly account for it."

The mother turned away with a low moan.

"There is nothing more that you can do?" asked the colonel.

"I have done all that I can," replied Carruthers.

"She will not last long?"

"It may be a matter of hours, or only minutes," he replied. "She is in excellent hands, however. No one could do more for her than Dr. Baldwin."

The two nurses whom Custer had arranged for had arrived, and when Dr. Carruthers departed he took his own nurse with him.

It was afternoon when deputies from the sheriff's and coroner's offices arrived from Los Angeles, together with detectives from the district attorney's office. Crumb's body still lay where it had fallen, guarded by a constable from the village of Ganado. It was surrounded by members of his company, villagers, and near-by ranchers, for word of the murder had spread rapidly in the district in that seemingly mysterious way in which news travels in rural communities. Among the crowd was Slick Allen, who had returned to the valley after his release from the county jail.

When the body was finally lifted from its resting place, and placed in the ambulance that had been brought from Los Angeles, one of the detectives picked up a horseshoe that had lain underneath the body. From its appearance it was evident that it had been upon a horse's hoof very recently, and had been torn off by force.

As the detective examined the shoe, several of the crowd pressed forward to look at it. Among them was Allen.

"That's off young Pennington's horse," he said.

"How do you know that?" inquired the detective.

"I used to work for them—took care of their saddle horses. This young Pennington's horse forges. They had to shoe him special, to keep him from pulling off the fore shoe. I could tell one of his shoes in a million. If they haven't walked all over his tracks I can tell whether that horse had been up here or not."

He stooped and examined the ground close to where the body had lain.

"There!" he said, pointing. "There's an imprint of one of his hind feet. See how the toe of that shoe is squared off? That was made by the Apache, all right!"

The detective was interested. He studied the hoofprint carefully, and searched for others, but this was the only one he could find.

"Looks like some one had been sweeping this place with a broom," he remarked. "There ain't much of anything shows."

A pimply-faced young man spoke up.

"There was some one sweeping the ground this morning," he said. "About five o'clock this morning I seen a girl dragging the branch of a tree after her, and sweeping along the road below here."

"Did you know her?" asked the detective.

"No—I never seen her before."

"Would you know her if you saw her again?"

"Sure I'd know her! She was a pippin. I'd know her horse, too."

CHAPTER XXXV

Eva was still breathing faintly as the sun dropped behind the western hills. Shannon had not left the house all day. She felt that Custer needed her, that they all needed her, however little she could do to mitigate their grief. There was at least a sense of sharing their burden, and her fine sensibilities told her that this service of love was quite as essential as the more practical help that she would have been glad to offer had it been within her power.

She was standing in the patio with Custer, at sunset, within call of Eva's room, as they all had been during the entire day, when a car drove up along the south drive and stopped at the patio entrance. Three of the four men in it alighted and advanced toward them.

"You are Custer Pennington?" one of them asked.

Pennington nodded.

"And you are Miss Burke— Miss Shannon Burke?"

"I am."

"I am a deputy-sheriff. I have a warrant here for your arrest."

"Arrest!" exclaimed Custer. "For what?"

He read the warrant to them. It charged them with the murder of Wilson Crumb.

"I am sorry, Mr. Pennington," said the deputy sheriff; "but I have been given these warrants, and there is nothing for me to do but serve them."

"You have to take us away now? Can't you wait—until—my sister is dying in there. Couldn't it be arranged so that I could stay here under arrest as long as she lives?"

The deputy shook his head.

"It would be all right with me," he said; "but I have no authority to let you stay. I'll telephone in, though, and see what I can do. Where is the telephone?"

Pennington told him.

"You two stay here with my men," said the deputy sheriff, "while I telephone."

He was gone about fifteen minutes. When he returned, he shook his head.

"Nothing doing," he said. "I have to bring you both in right away."

"May I go to her room and see her again before I leave?" asked Custer.

"Yes," said the deputy; but when Custer turned toward his sister's room, the officer accompanied him.

Dr. Baldwin and one of the nurses were in the room. Young Pennington came and stood beside the bed, looking down on the white face and the tumbled curls upon the pillow. He could not perceive the slightest indication of life, yet they told him that Eva still lived. He knelt and kissed her, and then turned away. He tried to say good-bye to her, but his voice broke, and he turned and left the room hurriedly.

Colonel and Mrs. Pennington were in the patio, with Shannon and the officers. The colonel and his wife had just learned of this new blow, and both were stunned. The colonel seemed to have aged a generation in that single day. He was a tired, hopeless old man. The heart of his boy and that of Shannon Burke went out to him and to the suffering mother from whom their son to be taken at this moment in their lives when they needed him most. In their compassion for the older Penningtons they almost forgot the seriousness of their own situation.

At their arraignment next morning, the preliminary hearing was set for the following Friday. Early in the morning Custer had received word from Ganado that Eva still lived, and that Dr. Baldwin now believed they might hold some slight hope for her recovery.

At Ganado, despair and anxiety had told heavily upon the Penningtons. The colonel felt that he should be in Los Angeles, to assist in the defense of his son; and yet he knew that his place was with his wife, whose need of him was even greater. Nor would his heart permit him to leave the daughter whom he worshiped, so long as even a faint spark of life remained in that beloved frame.

Mrs. Evans returned from Los Angeles the following day. She was almost prostrated by this last of a series of tragedies ordered, as it seemed, by some malignant fate for the wrecking of her happiness. She told them that Guy appeared to be hopelessly insane. He did not know his mother, nor did he give the slightest indication of any recollection of his past life, or of the events that had overthrown his reason.

At ten o'clock on Wednesday night Dr. Baldwin came into the living room, where the colonel and his wife were sitting with Mrs. Evans. For two days none of them had been in bed. They were tired and haggard, but not more so than the old doctor, who had remained constantly on duty from the moment when he was summoned. Never had man worked with more indefatigable zeal than he to wrest a young life from the path of the grim reaper. There were deep lines beneath his eyes, and his face was pale and drawn, as he entered the room and stood before them; but for the first time in many hours there was a smile upon his lips.

"I believe," he said, "that we are going to save her."

The others were too much affected to speak. So long had hope been denied that now they dared not even think of hope.

"She regained consciousness a few moments ago. She looked up at me and smiled, and then she fell asleep. She is breathing quite naturally now. She must not be disturbed, though. I think it would be well if you all retired. Mrs. Pennington, you certainly must get some sleep—and you too, Mrs. Evans, or I cannot be responsible for the results. I have left word with the night nurse to call me immediately, if necessary, and if you will all go to your rooms I will lie on the sofa here in the living room. I feel at last that it will be safe for me to leave her in the hands of the nurse, and a little sleep won't hurt me."

The colonel took his old friend by the hand.

"Baldwin," he said, "it is useless to try to thank you. I couldn't, even if there were words to do it with."

"You don't have to, Pennington. I think I love her as much as you do. There isn't any one who knows her who doesn't love her, and who wouldn't have done as much as I. Now, get off to bed all of you, and I think we'll find something to be very happy about in the morning. If there is any change for the worst, I will let you know immediately."

In the county jail in Los Angeles, Custer Pennington and Shannon Burke, awaiting trial on charges of a capital crime, were filled with increasing happiness, as the daily reports from Ganado brought word of Eva's steady improvement, until at last that she was entirely out of danger.

The tedious preliminaries of selecting a jury were finally concluded. As witness after witness was called, Pennington came to realize for the first time what a web of circumstantial evidence the State had fabricated about him. Even from servants whom he knew to be loyal and friendly the most damaging evidence was elicited. His mother's second maid testified that she had seen him fully dressed in his room late in the evening before the murder, when she had come in, as was her custom, with a pitcher of iced water, not knowing that the young man was there. She had seen him lying upon the bed, with his gun in its holster hanging from the belt about his waist.

She also testified that the following morning, when she had come in to make up his bed, she had discovered that it had not been slept in.

The stableman testified that the Apache had been out on the night of the murder. He had rubbed the animal down earlier in the evening, when the defendant had come in from riding. At that time the two had examined the horse's shoes, the animal having just been reshod. He said that on the morning after the murder there were saddle sweat marks on the Apache's back, and that the off fore shoe was missing.

One of the K.K.S. employees testified that a young man, whom he partially identified as Custer, had ridden into their camp about nine o'clock on the night of the murder, and had inquired concerning the whereabouts of Crumb. He said that the young man seemed excited, and upon being told that Crumb was away he had ridden off rapidly toward Sycamore Canyon.

Added to all this were the damaging evidence of the detective who had found the Apache's off fore shoe under Crumb's body, and the positive identification of the shoe by Allen. The one thing that was lacking—a motive for the crime—was supplied by Allen and the Penningtons' house man.

The latter testified that among his other duties was the care of the hot water heater in the basement of the Pennington home. Upon the evening of Saturday, August 5, he had forgotten to shut off the burner, as was his custom. He had returned about nine o'clock, to do so. When he had left the house by the passageway leading from the basement beneath the south drive and opening on the hillside just above the water gardens, he had seen a man standing by the upper pool, with his arms about a woman, whom he was kissing. It was a bright moonlight night, and the house man had recognized the two as Custer Pennington and Miss Burke. Being embarrassed by having thus accidentally come upon them, he had moved away quietly in the opposite direction, among the shadows of the trees, and had returned to the bunk house.

The connecting link between this evidence and the motive for the crime was elicited from Allen in half an hour of direct examination, which constituted the most harrowing ordeal that Shannon Burke had ever endured; for it laid bare before the world, and before the man she loved, the sordid history of her life with Wilson Crumb. It portrayed her as a drug addict and a wanton; but, more terrible still, it established a motive for the murder of Crumb by Custer Pennington.

Owing to the fact that he had lain in a drunken stupor during the night of the crime, that no one had seen him from the time when the maid entered his room to bring his iced water until his father had found him fully clothed upon his bed at five o'clock the following morning, young Pennington was unable to account for his actions, or to state his whereabouts at the time when the murder was committed.

He realized what the effect of the evidence must be upon the minds of the jurors when he himself was unable to assert positively, even to himself, that he had not left his room that night. Nor was he very anxious to refute the charge against him, since in his heart he believed that Shannon Burke had killed Crumb. He did not even take the stand in his own defense.

The evidence against Shannon was less convincing. A motive, had been established in Crumb's knowledge of her past life and the malign influence that he had had upon it. The testimony of the camp flunky, who had seen her obliterating what evidence the trail might have given in the form of hoofprints constituted practically the only direct evidence that was brought against her. It seemed to Custer that the gravest charge that could justly be brought against her was that of accessory after the fact, provided the jury was convinced of his guilt.

Many witnesses testified, giving evidence concerning apparently irrelevant subjects. It was brought out, however, that Crumb died from the effects of a wound inflicted by a forty-five caliber pistol, that Custer Pennington possessed such a weapon, and that at the time of his arrest it had been found in its holster, with its cartridge belt, thrown carelessly upon the bed.

When Shannon Burke took the stand, all eyes were riveted upon her. They were attracted not only by her youth and beauty, but also by the morbid interest which the frequenters of court rooms would naturally feel in the disclosure of the life she had led at Hollywood. Even to the most sophisticated it appeared incredible that this refined girl, whose, soft well modulated voice and quiet manner carried a conviction of innate modesty, could be the woman whom Slick Allen's testimony had revealed in such a role of vice and degradation.

Allen's eyes were fastened upon her with the same intent and searching expression that had marked his attitude upon the occasion of his last visit to the Vista del Paso bungalow, as if he were trying to recall the identity of some half forgotten face.

Though Shannon gave her evidence in a simple, straightforward manner, it was manifest that she was undergoing an intense nervous strain. The story that she told, coming as it did out of a clear sky, unguessed either by the prosecution or by the defense, proved a veritable bombshell to them both. It came after it had appeared that the last link had been forged in the chain that fixed guilt upon Custer Pennington. She had asked, then, to be permitted to take the stand and tell her story in her own way.

"I did not see Mr. Crumb," she said, "from the time I left Hollywood on the 30th of July last year, until the afternoon before he was killed; nor had I communicated with him during that time. What Mr. Allen told you about my having been a drug addict was true, but he did not tell you that Crumb made me what I was, or that after I came to Ganado to live I overcame the habit. I did not live with Crumb as his wife. I was afraid of him, and did not want to go back to him. When I left, I did not even let him know where I was going.

"The afternoon before he was killed I met him accidentally in the patio of Colonel Pennington's home. The Penningtons had no knowledge of my association with Crumb. I knew that they wouldn't have tolerated me, had they known what I had been. Crumb demanded that I should return to him, and threatened to expose me if I refused. I knew that he was going to be up in the canyon that night. I rode up there and shot him. The next morning I went back and attempted to obliterate the tracks of my horse, for I had learned from Custer Pennington that it is sometimes easy to recognize individual peculiarities in the tracks of a shod horse. That is all, except that Mr.

Pennington had no knowledge of what I did and no part in it."

Momentarily her statement seemed to overthrow the State's case against Pennington; but that the district attorney was not convinced of its truth was indicated by his cross-examination of her and other witnesses, and later by the calling of new witnesses. They could not shake her testimony, but on the other hand she was unable to prove that she had ever possessed a forty-five-caliber pistol, or to account for what she had done with it after the crime.

During the course of her cross-examination many apparently unimportant and irrelevant facts were adduced, among them the name of the Middle Western town in which she had been born. This trivial bit of testimony was the only point that seemed to make any impression on Allen. Any one watching him at the moment would have seen a sudden expression of incredulity and consternation overspread his face, the hard lines of which slowly gave place to what might, in another, have suggested a semblance of grief.

For several minutes he sat staring at Shannon. Then he crossed to the side of her attorney, and whispered a few words in the lawyer's ear. Receiving an assent to whatever his suggestion might have been, he left the court room.

On the following day the defense introduced a new witness in the person of a Japanese who had been a house servant in the bungalow on the Vista del Paso. His testimony substantiated Shannon Burke's statement that she and Crumb had not lived together as man and wife.

Then Allen was recalled to the stand. He told of the last evening that he had spent at Crumb's bungalow, and of the fact that Miss Burke, who was then known to him as Gaza de Lure, had left the house at the same time he did. He testified that Crumb had asked her why she was going home so early; that she had replied that she wanted to write a letter; that he, Allen, had remarked "I thought you lived here," to which she had replied. "I'm here nearly all day, but I go home nights." The witness added that this conversation took place in Crumb's presence, and that the director did not in any way deny the truth of the girl's assertion.

Why Allen should have suddenly espoused her cause was a mystery to Shannon, only to be accounted for upon the presumption that if he could lessen the value of that part of her testimony which had indicated a possible motive for the crime, he might thereby strengthen the case against Pennington, toward whom he still felt enmity, and whom he had long ago threatened to "get."

The district attorney, in his final argument, drew a convincing picture of the crime from the moment when Custer Pennington saddled his horse at the stables at Ganado. He followed him up the canyon to the camp in Jackknife, where he had inquired concerning Crumb, and then down to Sycamore again, where, at the mouth of Jackknife, the lights of Crumb's car would have been visible up the larger canyon.

He demonstrated clearly that a man familiar with the hills, and searching for some one whom sentiments of jealousy and revenge were prompting him to destroy, would naturally investigate this automobile light that was shining where no automobile should be. That the prisoner had ridden out with the intention of killing Crumb was apparent from the fact that he had carried a pistol in a country where, under ordinary circumstances, there was no necessity for carrying a weapon of self-defense. He vividly portrayed the very instant of the commission of the crime—how Pennington leaned from his saddle and shot Crumb through the heart; the sudden leap of the murderer's horse as he was startled by the report of the pistol, or possibly by the falling body of the murdered man; and how, in so doing, he had forged and torn off the shoe that had been found beneath Crumb's body.

"And," he said, "this woman knew that he was going to kill Wilson Crumb. She knew it, and she made no effort to prevent it. On the contrary, as soon as it was light enough, she rode directly to the spot where Crumb's body lay, and, as has been conclusively demonstrated by the unimpeachable testimony of an eye witness, she deliberately sought to expunge all traces of her lover's guilt."

He derided Shannon's confession, which he termed an eleventh hour effort to save a guilty man from the gallows.

"If she killed Wilson Crumb, what did she kill him with?"

He picked up the bullet that had been extracted from Crumb's body.

"Where is the pistol from which this bullet came? Here it is, gentlemen!"

He picked up the weapon that had been taken from Custer's room.

"Compare this bullet with those others that were taken from the clip in the handle of this automatic. They are identical. This pistol did not belong to Shannon Burke. It was never in her possession. No pistol of this character was ever in her possession. Had she had one, she could have told where she obtained it, and whether it had been sold to her or to another; and the records of the seller would show whether or not she spoke the truth. Failing to tell us where she had disposed of it. She can do neither, and the reason which she cannot is because she never owned a forty-five caliber pistol. She never had one in her possession, and therefore she could not have killed Crumb with one."

When at length the case went to the jury, Custer Pennington's conviction seemed a foregone conclusion, while the fate of Shannon Burke was yet in the laps of the gods. The testimony that Allen and the Japanese servant had given in substantiation of Shannon's own statement that her relations with Wilson Crumb had only been those of an accomplice in the disposal of narcotics, removed from consideration the principal motive that she might have had for killing Crumb.

And so there was no great surprise when, several hours later, the jury returned a verdict in accordance with the public opinion of Los Angeles—where, owing to the fact that murder juries are not isolated, such cases are tried largely by the newspapers and the public. They found Custer Pennington, Jr., guilty of murder in the first degree, and Shannon Burke not guilty.

CHAPTER XXXVI

on the day when Custer was to be sentenced, Colonel Pennington and Shannon Burke were present in the court room. Mrs. Pennington had remained at home with Eva, who was slowly convalescing. Shannon reached the court room before the colonel. When he arrived, he sat down beside her, and placed his hand on hers.

"Whatever happens," he said, "we shall still believe in him. No matter what the evidence—and I do not deny that the jury brought in a just verdict in accordance with it— I know that he is innocent. He told me yesterday that he was innocent, and my boy would not lie to me. He thought that you killed Crumb, Shannon. He overheard the conversation between you and Crumb in the patio that day, and he knew that you had good reason to kill the man. He knows now, as we all know, that you did not. Probably it must always remain a mystery. He would not tell me that he was innocent until after you had been proven so. He loves you very much, my girl!"

"After all that he heard here in court? After what I have been? I thought none of you would ever want to see me again."

The colonel pressed her hand.

"Whatever happens," he said, "you are going back home with me. You tried to give your life for my son. If this were not enough, the fact that he loves you, and that we love you, is enough."

Two tears crept down Shannon's cheek—the first visible signs of emotion that she had manifested during all the long weeks of the ordeal that she had been through. Nothing had so deeply affected her as the magnanimity of the proud old Pennington, whose pride and honor, while she had always admired them, she had regarded as an indication of a certain puritanical narrowness that could not forgive the transgression of a woman.

When the judge announced the sentence, and they realized that Custer Pennington was to pay the death penalty, although it had been almost a foregone conclusion, the shock left them numb and cold.

Neither the condemned man nor his father gave any outward indication of the effect of the blow. They were Penningtons, and the Pennington pride permitted them no show of weakness before the eyes of strangers. Nor yet was there any bravado in their demeanor. The younger Pennington did not look at his father or Shannon as he was led away toward the cell, between two bailiffs.

As Shannon Burke walked from the court room with the colonel, she could think of nothing but the fact that in two months the man she loved was to be hanged. She tried to formulate plans for his release—wild, quixotic plans; but she could not concentrate her mind upon anything but the bewildering thought that in two months they would hang him by the neck until he was dead.

She knew that he was innocent. Who, then, had, committed the crime? Who had murdered Wilson Crumb?

Outside the Hall of Justice she was accosted by Allen, whom she attempted to pass without noticing. The colonel turned angrily on the man. He was in the mood to commit murder himself; but Allen forestalled any outbreak on the old man's part by a pacific gesture of his hands and a quick appeal to Shannon.

"Just a moment, please," he said. "I know you think I had a lot to do with Pennington's conviction. I want to help you now. I can't tell you why. I don't believe he was guilty. I changed my mind recently. If I can see you alone, Miss Burke. I can tell you something that might give you a line on the guilty party."

"Under no conceivable circumstances can you see Miss Burke alone," snapped the colonel.

"I'm not going to hurt her," said Allen. "Just let her talk to me here alone on the sidewalk, where no one can overhear."

"Yes," said the girl, who could see no opportunity pass which held the slightest ray of hope for Custer.

The colonel walked away, but turned and kept his eyes on the man when he was out of earshot. Allen spoke hurriedly to the girl for ten or fifteen minutes, and then turned and left her. When she returned to the colonel the latter did not question her. When she did not offer to confide in him, he knew that she must have good reasons for her reticence, since he realized that her sole interest lay in aiding Custer.

For the next two months the colonel divided his time between Ganado and San Francisco, that he might be near San Quentin, where Custer was held pending the day of execution. Mrs. Pennington, broken in health by the succession of blows that she had sustained, was sorely in need of his companionship and help. Eva was rapidly regaining her strength and some measure of her spirit. She had begun to realize how useless and foolish her attempt at self-destruction had been, and to see that the braver and nobler course would have been to give Guy the benefit of her moral support in his time of need.

The colonel, who had wormed from Custer the full story of his conviction upon the liquor charge, was able to convince her that Guy had not played a dishonorable part, and that of the two he had suffered more than Custer. Her father did not condone or excuse Guy's wrong-doing, but he tried to make her understand that it was no indication of a criminal inclination, but rather the thoughtless act of an undeveloped boy.

During the two months they saw little or nothing of Shannon. She remained in Los Angeles, and when she made the long trip to San Quentin to see Custer, or when they chanced to see her, they could not but note how thin and drawn she was becoming. The roses had left her cheeks, and there were deep lines beneath her eyes, in which there was constantly an expression of haunting fear.

As the day of the execution drew nearer, the gloom that had hovered over Ganado for months settled like a dense pall upon them all. On the day before the execution the colonel left for San Francisco, to say good-bye to his son for the last time. Custer had insisted that his mother and Eva must not come, and they had acceded to his wish.

On the afternoon when the colonel arrived at San Quentin, he was permitted to see his son for the last time. The two conversed in low tones, Custer asking questions about his mother and sister, and about the little everyday activities of the ranch. Neither of them referred to the event of the following morning.

"Has Shannon been here today?" the colonel asked.

Custer shook his head.

"I haven't seen her this week," he said. "I suppose she dreaded coming. I don't blame her. I should like to have seen her once more, though!"

Presently they stood in silence for several moments.

"You'd better go, dad," said the boy. "Go back to mother and Eva. Don't take it too hard. It isn't so bad, after all. I have led a bully life, and I have never forgotten once that I am a Pennington. I shall not forget it tomorrow. "

The father could not speak. They clasped hands once, the older man turned away, and the guards led Custer back to the death cell for the last time.

CHAPTER XXXVII

It was morning when the colonel reached the ranch. He found his wife and Eva sitting in Custer's room. They knew the hour, and they were waiting there to be as near him as they could. They were weeping quietly. In the kitchen across the patio they could hear Hannah sobbing.

They sat there for a long time in silence. Suddenly they heard a door slam in the patio, and the sound of someone running.

"Colonel Pennington! Colonel Pennington!" a voice cried.

The colonel stepped to the door of Custer's room. It was the bookkeeper calling him.

"What is it?" he asked. "Here I am."

"The Governor has granted a stay of execution. There is new evidence. Miss Burke is on her way here now. She has found the man who killed Crumb!"

What more he said the colonel did not hear, for he had turned back into the room, and, collapsing on his son's bed, had broken into tears—he who had gone through those long weeks like a man of iron.

It was nearly noon before Shannon arrived. She had been driven from Los Angeles by an attaché of the district attorney's office. The Penningtons had been standing on the east porch, watching the road with binoculars, so anxious were they for confirmation of their hopes.

She was out of the car before it had stopped and was running toward them. The man who had accompanied her followed, and joined them on the porch. Shannon threw her arms around Mrs. Pennington's neck.

"He is safe!" she cried. "Another has confessed, and has satisfied the district attorney of his guilt."

"Who was it?" they asked.

Shannon turned toward Eva.

"It is going to be another blow to you all," she said; "but wait until I'm through, and you will understand that it could not have been otherwise. It was Guy who killed Wilson Crumb."

"Guy? Why should he have done it?"

"That was it. That was why suspicion was never directed toward him. Only he knew the facts that prompted him to commit the deed. It was Allen who suggested to me the possibility that it might have been Guy. I have spent nearly two months at the sanatorium with this gentleman from the district attorney's office, in an effort to awaken Guy's sleeping intellect to a realization of the past, and of the present necessity for recalling it. He has been improving steadily, but it was only yesterday that memory returned to him. We worked on the theory that if he could be made to realize that Eva lived, the cause of his mental sickness would be removed. We tried everything, and we had almost given up hope when, almost like a miracle his memory returned, while he was looking at a snapshot of Eva that I had shown him. The rest was easy, especially after he knew that she had recovered. Instead of the necessity for confession resulting in a further shock, it seemed to inspirit him. His one thought was of Custer, his one hope that we would be in time to save him."

"Why did he kill Crumb?" asked Eva.

"Because Crumb killed Grace. He told me the whole story yesterday."

Very carefully Shannon related all that Guy had told of Crumb's relations with his sister, up to the moment of Grace's death.

"I am glad he killed him!" said Eva. "I would have had no respect for him if he hadn't done it."

"Guy told me that the evening before he killed Crumb he had been looking over a motion picture magazine, and he had seen there a picture of Crumb which tallied with the photograph he had taken from Grace's dressing table— a portrait of the man who, as she told him, was responsible for her trouble. Guy had never been able to learn this man's identity, but the picture in the magazine, with his name below it, was a reproduction of the same photograph. There was no question as to the man's identity. The scarf-pin, and a lock of hair falling in a peculiar way over the forehead, marked the pictures as identical. Though Guy had never seen Crumb, he knew from conversations that he had heard here that it was Wilson Crumb who was directing the picture that was to be taken on Ganado. He immediately got his pistol, saddled his horse, and rode up to the camp in search of Crumb. It was he whom one of the witnesses mistook for Custer. He then did what the district attorney attributed to Custer. He rode to the mouth of Jackknife, and saw the lights of Crumb's car up near El Camino Largo. While he was in Jackknife, Eva must have ridden down Sycamore from her meeting with Crumb, passing Jackknife before Guy rode back into Sycamore. He rode up to where Crumb was attempting to crank his engine. Evidently the starter had failed to work, for Crumb was standing in front of the car, in the glare of the headlights, attempting to crank it. Guy accosted him, charged him with the murder of Grace, and shot him. He then started for home by way of El Camino Largo. Half a mile up the trail he dismounted and hid his pistol and belt in a hollow tree. Then he rode home.

"He told me that while he never for an instant regretted his act, he did not sleep all that night, and was in a highly nervous condition when the shock of Eva's supposed death unbalanced his mind; otherwise he would gladly have assumed the guilt of Crumb's death at the time when Custer and I were accused.

"After we had obtained Guy's confession, Allen gave us further information tending to prove Custer's innocence. He said he could not give it before without incriminating himself; and as he had no love for Custer, he did not intend to hang for a crime he had not committed. He knew that he would surely hang if he confessed the part that he had played in formulating the evidence against Custer.

"Crumb had been the means of sending Allen to the county jail, after robbing him of several thousand dollars. The day before Crumb was killed, Allen's sentence expired. The first thing he did was to search for Crumb, with the intention of killing the man. He learned at the studio where Crumb was, and he followed him immediately. He was hanging around the camp out of sight, waiting for Crumb, when he heard the shot that killed him. His investigation led him to Crumb's body. He was instantly overcome by the fear, induced by his guilty conscience, that the crime would be laid at his door. In casting about for some plan by which he might divert suspicion from himself, he discovered an opportunity to turn it against a man whom he hated. The fact that he had been a stableman on Ganado, and was familiar with the customs of the ranch made it an easy thing for him to go to the stables, saddle the Apache, and ride him up Sycamore to Crumb's body. Here he deliberately pulled the off fore shoe from the horse and hit it under Crumb's body. Then he rode back to the stable, unsaddled the Apache, and made his way to the village.

"The district attorney said that we need have no fear but that Custer will be exonerated and freed. And, Eva"—she turned to the girl with a happy smile—"I have it very confidentially that there is small likelihood that any jury in southern California will convict Guy, if he bases his defense upon a plea of insanity."

Eva smiled bravely and said:

"One thing I don't understand, Shannon, is what you were doing brushing the road with a bough from a tree, on the morning after the killing of Crumb, if you weren't trying to obliterate some one's tracks."

"That's just what I was trying to do," said Shannon. "Ever since Custer taught me something about tracking, it has held a certain fascination for me, so that I often try to interpret the tracks I see along the trails in the hills. It was because of this, I suppose, that I immediately recognized the Apache's tracks around the body of Crumb. I immediately jumped to the conclusion that Custer had killed him, and I did what I could to remove this evidence. As it turned out, my efforts did more harm than good, until Allen's explanation cleared up the matter."

"And why," asked the colonel, "did Allen undergo this sudden change of heart?"

Shannon turned toward him, her face slightly flushed, though she looked him straight in the eyes as she spoke.

"It is a hard thing for me to tell you," she said.

"Allen is a bad man—a very bad man; yet in the worst of men there is a spark of good. Allen told me this morning, in the district attorney's office, what it was that had kindled to life the spark of good in him. He is my father."

THE END...